Lurlene McDaniel

angels in pink

Kathleen's Story

Delacorte  Press

*This book is lovingly dedicated to
Jedidiah McDaniel.*

*I would like to express my gratitude
to Jan Hamilton Powell and Mickey Milita of
Erlanger Medical Center, Baroness Campus,
for their invaluable help in shaping this series.*

Published by
Delacorte Press
an imprint of
Random House Children's Books
a division of Random House, Inc.
New York

Visit us on the Web! www.randomhouse.com/teens
Educators and librarians, for a variety of teaching tools, visit us at
www.randomhouse.com/teachers

Library of Congress Cataloging-in-Publication Data
McDaniel, Lurlene.
Kathleen's story / Lurlene McDaniel.
p. cm.—(Angels in pink)
Summary: With the support of her two best friends, sixteen-year-old
Kathleen tries to balance her summer volunteer work at the hospital with
her responsibilities caring for her mother, who has multiple sclerosis, and
her attraction to a handsome boy.
ISBN 0-385-73156-6 (trade) — ISBN 0-385-90193-3 (GLB)
[1. Family problems—Fiction. 2. Interpersonal relations—Fiction.
3. Hospitals—Fiction. 4. Multiple sclerosis—Fiction. 5. Mothers and
daughters—Fiction. 6. Christian life—Fiction. 7. Florida—Fiction.] I. Title.
PZ7.M4784172Kat 2004
[Fic]—dc22
2004009955

The text of this book is set in 11-point Goudy.

Book design by Michelle Gengaro

Printed in the United States of America

December 2004

10 9 8 7 6 5 4 3 2 1

BTP

Angels in Pink Volunteer's Creed

I will pass through this life but once.
If there is any kindness I can show, any good that I
can do, any comfort that I can offer, let me do it
now, for one day I will be gone and what
will remain is the memory of what I did for others.

one

"ARE WE READY?" Raina St. James asked. She looked expectantly at her two friends.

"I'm ready," Holly Harrison answered. *More than ready*, she thought. Anything to get herself out of the house and away from her parents' eagle eyes, especially her father's. His will was impossible to bend, his mind impossible to change. He treated her like she was twelve instead of sixteen, so yes, she was ready for Raina's project.

"I'm ready too," Kathleen McKensie said, knowing it was a lie. She wanted to say, *I don't even want to be here*, but she didn't have the guts. This summer project was totally Raina's idea, but because she'd let her two friends talk her into it, she had no one to blame but herself for agreeing to join them.

They climbed out of Raina's car and she locked the doors with the electronic key. "This is going to be a great summer," Raina said. "Trust me."

"Don't we always?" Holly said.

The three of them, friends since sixth grade, had just finished their sophomore year at Cummings High in Tampa, Florida, where they were practically inseparable. But it was Raina who led them—not in a bossy way, but by sheer force of personality and persuasion. Once Raina set her mind on something, it came to pass, and from the moment she'd started talking about Parker-Sloan General Hospital's summer volunteer program after the Christmas break, Kathleen had known she'd cave and join Raina and Holly as a volunteer. However, now that the day was really upon them, Kathleen was wishing she'd voiced her objections when she'd had the chance. For starters, being a volunteer would consume her entire summer. And then, of course, she had to consider her mother, whom she decided not to think about at the moment.

Kathleen followed Raina and Holly through the parking garage to the elevator. It was only eight on a Saturday morning, but already heat was starting to build. By noon, it would be in the high eighties. They should have been heading to the pool at Raina's townhome complex for some sun worship instead of to volunteer orientation at the hospital.

"What floor?" Holly asked once the elevator door slid open and they stepped inside.

Raina said, "Third."

Holly pushed the button and the elevator

rose. "This place is the size of a small city. I'll never find my way around."

"Sure you will," Raina countered. "I'll help both of you." Raina's mother was head of nursing at Parker-Sloan, so Raina knew plenty about the layout of the giant hospital complex, which easily covered two city blocks. She was fascinated by the world of medicine and today she was starting as a teen volunteer, fulfilling a dream she'd had for years, and having her two best friends with her made it even more special.

"Gee, thanks," Kathleen said with an edge of sarcasm. Although Kathleen understood Raina's fascination, she was *not* attracted to medicine. No way. And she secretly thought that Raina wouldn't be either if she had a sick mother at home as Kathleen did. As for Holly, Kathleen knew she'd do anything to escape her strict parents. That fact, and the fact that Raina was dating Holly's brother, Hunter, made Holly more agreeable to Raina's wishes.

"What are friends for?" Raina said, flashing a perky smile. The elevator stopped and the girls stepped into a hallway. "The auditorium is this way," Raina said, pointing left.

As they rounded a corner, Kathleen saw a line of teens filing through open double wooden doors—mostly girls, but some boys too. Inside the doors, stadium-style seats with flip-up writing desks made a sharp downward descent. At the bottom were a desk and a blackboard that stretched across the wall. A man and woman were watching the group file in and waving them toward the front. "Don't be shy," the man called. "Come on down."

"Looks like we're not the only volunteers who signed up," Holly said over her shoulder.

"Told you so," Raina said. "This is one of the best places in the city to spend a summer. Plus, don't forget, if we make it through this program, we can sign up to be year-round volunteers and earn credits toward graduation."

"Which is better than another science class," Holly said.

"But no money," Kathleen added pointedly. She'd given up a part-time job in a clothing boutique because of the program.

"Hence the term 'volunteer,' " Raina said, not a bit apologetic about Kathleen's job loss.

"Well, I think it's going to be fun." Holly took a seat along with her friends.

"And so will you, Kathleen." Raina gave her friend a patronizing pat that almost made Kathleen get up and leave. She might have too, if the man standing at the front of the room hadn't started talking.

"Welcome, summer volunteers, to our Pink Angels program orientation. I'm Mark Powell, director of volunteers at Parker-Sloan, and this is Connie Vasquez, volunteer coordinator." He nodded at the slim young dark-haired woman standing next to him. Connie waved. "All of you have passed the preliminary part of our Angels program in that first set of paperwork you submitted in April. Today"—he paused for dramatic effect—"more paperwork." He grinned, and Connie held up several thick file folders while the audience groaned.

"But after we fill out the forms and go over some rules," Connie added, "we'll break into small groups and take a tour of the hospital and the various floors and departments where you'll be used as volunteers. We'll meet here afterward for free pizza."

The audience applauded.

"One of the things in your packet is a form that asks for your shirt sizes, because all of you will be issued special shirts that will instantly identify you as an Angel volunteer to our staff and personnel," Connie said.

"Read the sheet about our dress code carefully, because there's no wiggle room there," Mark added. "The term 'Pink Angels' came from the pink shirts that our volunteers started wearing in the 1970s." He held up a pale pink polo shirt. "Then somewhere along the way, boys asked to join our program—nursing is a noble profession," he inserted with a grin. "So we added navy blue shirts. The guys just didn't feel comfortable in pink."

"You got *that* right," a guy called from a back row, making everyone laugh.

Mark held up his hands. "Now we mix the two shirt colors, so it doesn't matter what color you wear, but one must be worn *at all times* that you're on duty," he said. "Khaki or black slacks or skirts paired with the shirts is our uniform."

"I look lousy in a skirt," the same male voice said, causing another ripple of laughter.

"Who's the comedian?" Mark asked, craning his neck.

"That would be me, Carson Kiefer." A hand waved from the back.

Kathleen turned to see a good-looking boy with black hair and a flashy grin.

"Ah," Mark said with a nod, "Dr. Kiefer's son. Your father told me you'd be joining our program this summer."

The way he said it made Kathleen think there was more to the story of Carson's admittance to the program than was being said.

"I promised," Carson said with a snappy salute. "So here I am, signed, sealed and hogtied."

Mark rocked back on his heels and cleared his throat. "Well then, Connie, pass out the packets and let's get started."

After forty minutes of listening to Mark and Connie talk about the program, the rules and their expectations for the volunteers, Kathleen felt her head start to swim. When it was time to break into small groups, two assistants joined Mark and Connie, and the volunteers were asked to count off, then gather with the others of their same number for their tours. Kathleen found herself in Mark's group along with ten others, including the irrepressible Carson. He caught her eye and winked. She averted her gaze. *Show-off.*

Mark led them around the administrative floors first, explaining vital clerical duties that some volunteers would be assigned. That sounded safe to Kathleen—pushing paper and files would keep her away from sick people. As they walked, Mark said, "Lots of variety for you volunteers. Different departments will fill out request forms for your services, so you could be filing one day and distributing food trays on another. The nursing staff will use you a lot to transport patients to other parts of the hospital, for tests, treatments and discharge. All of you will be trained to move patients on stretchers and in wheelchairs."

Kathleen realized she was way ahead of the curve when it came to wheelchair transporting.

"Parker-Sloan manages about four thousand volunteers a week, both adults and teens. We're proud of our program and the people in it," Mark said when the group had been herded into the elevator and was heading toward the upper floors. "We really depend on our volunteers to free up staff for patient care. You're doing an important job."

Beside her, Kathleen heard Carson say, "Rah, rah," under his breath. She glanced at him and he flashed a sexy smile. She felt her cheeks color and quickly looked away.

The doors opened and Mark led them into a brightly painted hallway. "This is the children's wing. Most volunteers love pulling this assignment best."

The group followed Mark into a light-filled room lined with bookshelves and desks holding three computer terminals. An area rug dotted with beanbags and floor pillows faced a television set that was showing a cartoon with the sound turned down low. Several children were sitting at pint-size painted tables, along with several adults. The kids wore hospital-issue gowns and pj's in bright colors and cartoon prints. "The playroom," Mark said. The children didn't look sick to Kathleen. One boy had an arm in a sling. Another was propped up in a wheelchair, reading a book. Others were coloring or working puzzles. A small group were doing supervised finger painting.

"How's it going, Judy?" Mark asked one of the women.

"Fine. This your newest crop?"

"Handpicked," Mark said.

Judy greeted them. Kathleen heard several of

the girls murmur about how cute the kids were and how much they wanted to work on this floor. Except for occasionally babysitting the Thomas baby in her neighborhood, Kathleen hadn't spent much time around children, so she hoped she'd be assigned elsewhere.

"Your eyes aren't misting over," Carson whispered in her ear. "Don't you like kids?"

He so startled her that she stepped backward and almost fell over a chair. He grabbed her arm to steady her.

"You okay?" Mark asked as all eyes turned toward her. "Don't need one of our volunteers breaking her leg during orientation," he added with a smile.

The others laughed and Kathleen blushed furiously. "I'm fine." She pulled her arm from Carson's grasp.

"You're welcome," Carson said out loud, embarrassing her even more.

Back out in the hall, Kathleen scooted to the far side of the group, away from Carson, as Mark continued with his tour. "The babies are down that hall." He pointed.

"Will those kids in the playroom be all right?" one of the girls asked.

"All the kids on this wing will get well and go home. They come through with pneumonia, dehydration, compound fractures—things like that. Most don't stay long."

"Aren't we going in there?" another girl asked, gesturing at two large closed doors on the other side of the corridor.

"That's the pediatric oncology ward," Mark told the group. "Those kids are on chemo and range in age from five to sixteen. Many of them stay for long periods. We rarely put you summer volunteers in there because it's a sad place to work and not everyone's cut out for it."

Murmurs started again. Kathleen stared at the doors. Terminal illness. She shuddered.

Mark's tour took the better part of an hour and a half and threaded through most of the floors and wings of the giant hospital. By the time they returned to the auditorium where the orientation had begun, Kathleen felt more overwhelmed than ever by the size of the facility, and she wasn't alone. She heard others talking about it too. During the tour, they had seen the internal medicine clinic, the labor and delivery area, the new babies' nurseries, the medical library, intensive care units for several specialties, cardiac services, all of children's services, radiology, the kidney dialysis units, the oncology treatment rooms, the eye clinic, the oncology research and pathology departments, the surgical and operating room areas, the trauma unit, the emergency room, the cafeteria, the gift shop, the post office and the mailrooms. Her head spun. "Everyone will be issued maps and directions," Mark announced. "It won't take you long to figure out the place. Promise."

The scent of fresh pizza drifted from the auditorium. "Time to eat. We'll reconvene for questions," Mark said, and invited them to help themselves to the pizza sitting in boxes on long tables and the cans of soda in large coolers. Her group didn't need a second invitation and crowded around the tables. Kathleen went to the end of the line, waiting for her friends to return from their tours so they could eat together. She was reading some of the information in her welcome packet when she heard, "Hope you like cheese pizza."

She looked up to see Carson standing in front of her holding out a paper plate with a slice of pizza on it. "For me?" she asked.

"A peace offering," he said.

"Peace offering? For what?"

"I thought maybe you'd tell me what I've done to tick you off." He stood peering down at her, his dark eyes full of mischief. "So"—his gaze lingered on her name tag, pinned above her breast—"Kathleen McKensie, what have I done to tick you off?"

two

KATHLEEN FELT THE ever-familiar flush of red creeping up her neck and across her cheeks. "I—I don't know what you mean."

"Sure you do," Carson said. "You haven't given me one smile since we started out today. And I tried to get several out of you. I even rescued you from falling over and all that got me was you moving as far away from me as possible. I feel rejected and I don't know why."

She gave him a blank stare, uncertain how to react. His words rebuked, but his dark eyes teased. Was he flirting with her? Boys didn't flirt with her. They flirted with Raina, who was pretty but who had Hunter as a boyfriend so was never interested. They flirted with Holly, who giggled and acted like a kid at Christmas. But Kathleen? No—boys never came on to her. She'd sometimes thought it was her mane of deep red hair and freckles that turned them off, but as she got older, she'd decided it was because she was a social dud. She didn't know how to talk to boys. She didn't know how to flirt.

As her silence lengthened, Carson sighed. "Why don't you take this plate of pizza before I drop it, and come sit down with me."

"I—I'm not hungry." *Liar*, said her inner voice. She was starved. Or she had been starved until he came over to her. Where were her friends, anyway?

Carson rebalanced the plates—she saw now that he held two—then took her elbow and guided her to a desk chair several rows up from the crowded rows near the tables and set the plate in front of her. "Come on, eat it while it's still warm."

"You sound like my mother," she blurted.

"Well, I'm positive I don't *feel* like your mother."

She blushed and said, "You don't look like my mother either."

"Glad we settled that." He grinned. "So let's start with the simple stuff. Where do you go to school?"

She told him. "How about you?"

"Bryce Academy," he said, naming the most exclusive and prestigious school in the Tampa Bay area. "Not my choice." He sounded apologetic. "I was enrolled at birth."

"I've heard it's a good school." *What a lame thing to say.* She'd never been good at small talk.

He took a bite of his pizza. "I'm not exactly a stellar student. But then, I don't care." He leaned sideways in his chair. "But I'll bet you are, aren't you, Kathleen."

The way he said her name sent a shiver through her, which made her face redden again. "There's nothing wrong with making good grades."

"Right." He measured her with his sexy brown eyes. "So why did you volunteer to be a Pink Angel? Because you want to save the world?"

He made it sound as if being a do-gooder was not very cool, which irked her. "No. I joined because my two best friends made me."

He laughed. "I like your honesty, Kathleen."

"What about you? Are you into saving the world?" She almost added, *Because you sure don't look the type,* but instantly thought better of it. He had probably joined to meet girls.

"No way. I either wore an orange jumpsuit and picked up trash alongside the highway this summer or became a volunteer."

Her eyes widened. From all she'd read and heard, the program didn't take troublemakers. "But how—?"

"Friends in high places," he said, leaning so close that she smelled soap on his skin.

Her skin tingled. "Oh."

He straightened. "My parents are both cardiologists here. My older brother is starting his medical residency in Detroit, and my older sister, an ophthalmologist in Denver, is doing eye surgeries in Bosnia to help the downtrodden. You might say that the Kiefer clan is steeped in the brine of medicine. And good deeds."

Kathleen heard an undercurrent of bitterness in his voice, recognizing it because she had experienced the emotion herself. "And so you're a Pink Angel. Does that mean you're starting down a medical career path of your own?"

"Hardly."

"So, then, what *do* you want to be when you grow up?" She was being sarcastic, and Raina had warned her more than once about being sarcastic. *"Guys don't like to be put down."*

Her comment didn't seem to bother him. "Who says I have to grow up?" he asked.

"Why wouldn't you want to? It's what people do."

"I think being grown up is highly overrated and a lot less fun than I'm having now."

"Including picking up trash in an orange jumpsuit?" He was making her angry. She looked down at her pizza but had lost her appetite. With doctors for parents, a private school education and his pretty-boy good looks, he seemed arrogant.

"Would you fall for a guy wearing orange?"

"I wouldn't fall for a guy like you at all."

"Ouch," he said, slumping over as if he'd been shot.

Her face got hot again.

He straightened and looked her squarely in the eye. "You know, Kathleen, I think I'm going to have a much better time this summer than I'd planned on having."

"Why's that?"

His sexy grin emerged. "Because I've never been with you before. And from my vantage point, I think you're going to be a delicious experience."

Too stunned to respond, she watched him edge out of his seat, walk up the steps and leave the auditorium.

"Yoo-hoo! Earth calling Kathleen." Raina snapped her fingers in front of Kathleen's face, making her friend jump.

"Sorry!" Kathleen said, flushing. "I—I was lost in space."

Holly took Carson's seat. "Who's the hunk?"

"What?"

"The guy who was sitting here. Raina and I watched the two of you talking; then he got up and left and you got that vacant stare on your face. You didn't even see us come down the stairs. What did he say to you?"

"He's a jerk," Kathleen said, folding over her paper plate and squashing the uneaten pizza.

"It was that Kiefer guy, wasn't it?" Raina asked. "My mom knows his parents. They share an office in the hospital and do tons of heart surgeries. They're supposed to be really good."

"Well, their son's a conceited dope."

"Listen to that, Holly—he's got our best friend all shook up." Raina feigned shock.

"Don't tease me."

"Lighten up, Raina," Holly said, immediately sympathetic toward Kathleen. "Maybe he said something dirty. Did he? Did he make a crude pass?"

"All guys are crude," Raina said. "Except for my Hunter. He's a saint. Which is a problem too," she added as an afterthought.

"What did the guy say to you?" Holly persisted.

"He thinks knowing me will be 'delicious.' "

"Whoa, that qualifies as out of bounds," Raina said. "Want me to have him dumped from the summer program? I'll bet if I tell my mother, she can make it happen."

Kathleen shook her head. "He didn't say it in a crude way. It was more like a comment. You know, an observation."

Raina arched an eyebrow. "Maybe we should skip this pizza bash and go have a heart-to-heart at the Sub Shop." It was one of their favorite haunts.

"I'm for it," Holly said. "We may need to dissect the whole conversation. We might have to plan a strategy to help Kathleen deal with this guy."

Kathleen eyed the wall clock and sat bolt up-right. "Oh my gosh!" She grabbed for her purse and riffled through it. "I told my mother I'd be home by noon and it's one-thirty."

"So you're a little late. She knew you were coming to an orientation," Raina said.

"I'll bet she's called. I turned my phone on vi-brate so it wouldn't ring during the tour." She found her phone in her purse, looked at the dis-play and groaned. "Oh, yes. I have three missed calls." She started up the stairs. "Come on, Raina, drive me home."

"Your packet," Holly called.

"Bring it. I've got to get home right this minute."

"Wait," Raina called, scooping up her things.

Kathleen was rushing so fast that she tripped on the top step. "Hurry! Don't you understand? What if Mom's in trouble because I'm late!"

"Mom! I'm home," Kathleen called, dumping her belongings onto the table in the foyer. She turned and waved away Raina and Holly, still in the car.

Raina yelled, "I'll call you!" before driving off.

The house was cool and quiet. Fear made Kathleen's heart hammer. She hurried to the kitchen, where she found her mother sitting in her electric wheelchair, staring out the patio doors. She could tell that her mother had been crying. "Mom, are you all right?"

"I was scared," Mary Ellen McKensie said, sniffing back tears. "I—I thought something bad had happened to you."

"I'd turned my phone off. I'm sorry. The orientation took longer than I thought."

"You should have called. You know how I worry."

The chastisement irritated Kathleen. Her mother's fears were irrational and aimed to make Kathleen feel more guilty than she already did. "I said I was sorry. Have you eaten lunch?"

"I wasn't hungry. Just worried."

Kathleen took deep breaths to calm herself. "I left you a sandwich in the refrigerator before I left. All you had to do—"

"I wasn't hungry," her mother interrupted. "Have you eaten?"

"I was planning on having lunch with you," Kathleen lied. "If I eat with you now, will you be hungry?"

"Maybe." Her mother looked contrite. "If we eat together."

"Fine." Kathleen busied herself with preparing a second sandwich. In minutes she had put the food on the table and poured them each a glass of ice tea.

Her mother rolled her wheelchair to her spot

at the round kitchen table. "You should drink milk," she said.

"I don't want milk, Mom." Kathleen bit into her sandwich to keep words she might regret from spilling out of her mouth.

"How was the orientation?"

"Fine." Kathleen watched her mother pick up the sandwich on her plate with a shaking hand. "Do you want me to cut that any smaller for you?"

"I can manage." They ate in strained silence. "Do you think you'll like being a Pink Angel?"

Kathleen knew her mother was trying to say "I'm sorry," but at the moment, all she felt was anger toward her mother for acting helpless when she could do better, and anger at herself for getting distracted at the hospital and forgetting about her duties. "I have a stack of papers to go through, but yes, I think I'll be good at it. One of a volunteer's most important jobs is transporting patients around the hospital. I know how to do that really good, don't you think?"

"You've been transporting me for years. Would they like a reference?"

Kathleen offered a conciliatory smile. "Probably not."

"Do you know your hours? When you'll be working?"

"I'll have to go the same times as Holly and

Raina. Raina's really gung ho, so I imagine we'll do the max."

"You could drive our van."

Their family vehicle was a wheelchair-adapted van, a monster that Kathleen didn't like driving around town unless she had to. It had a special mechanical lift for loading her mother and the wheelchair, as well as special controls that her mother could use to drive it herself.

"You may need it," Kathleen said.

"I can't drive it without you."

"Sure you can. You did at Christmas."

"I've gotten worse since Christmas."

Kathleen wasn't sure that was true, but so long as her mother *thought* she couldn't do something, she wouldn't try. "Raina will drive. I'll go with her."

With their lunch finished, Mary Ellen said, "I feel light-headed. I should take a nap."

Kathleen followed the wheelchair into her mother's room. There she snapped on the chair's brakes, locked her arms around her mother's upper body from behind and helped her swing herself onto the bed. Kathleen covered her mother with a quilt sewn by her great-grandmother. "Get some rest."

"What will you do?"

"Call Raina. Read. Surf the Net. The usual stuff."

"You can order pizza if you don't want to cook tonight," her mother said.

"I'm kind of sick of pizza. I'd rather cook us something."

"All right." As Kathleen was about to close the bedroom door, her mother added, "I love you."

"I love you too, Mom."

Once the door was closed, Kathleen sagged against the wall. She missed going to school. At least it filled up her days. The volunteer program might turn out to be her salvation this summer after all. Besides, having to dash home from a volunteer job if her mother needed her would be a whole lot easier than leaving a paying job. She conjured up Carson's face and sexy grin. *Delicious*. He'd called her delicious. She wondered how yummy she'd be to him if he ever got a glimpse into her real life. A life dedicated to caring for a mother with multiple sclerosis.

three

KATHLEEN WAS LOST in a book when her phone rang. She answered and heard Raina's perky "Is everything all right?"

"Of course it is," Kathleen confessed with a sigh. "Mom was overreacting."

"She treats you like a slave."

"Raina . . . don't," Kathleen warned. This had been a sore point between them for years. Raina made no bones about her belief that Mary Ellen's helplessness was due in part to Kathleen's availability. Kathleen knew that while Raina was right about some of it, she wasn't right about all of it. Raina hadn't watched Mary Ellen deteriorate right before her eyes as Kathleen had. In the past ten years, from the time Kathleen was six, she had watched her mother go from having spastic tremors in her legs that caused her to fall to using a cane, then a walker and, finally, a wheelchair. And while her mother could stand and manage a shuffling kind of walk, the effort was painful. Kathleen saw her attempting it less and less.

"Sorry, sorry," Raina said quickly. "I'm not trying to hassle you. I'm just always wishing things were different for you."

"I wish things were different for my mother," Kathleen said. "I wish a lot of things." Her gaze automatically went to the large photograph of her father that she kept on her bedside table. Mary Ellen said that his smile and hers were twin images, stamped forever on Kathleen's face. Kathleen's father was dead, taken from them both when Kathleen was seven by a drunk driver who had struck their car, killing James McKensie instantly and sending Mary Ellen to the hospital in serious condition, where she remained for almost a month. Kathleen had been at home with a sitter, so she'd been spared, but the accident greatly accelerated the course of Mary Ellen's MS, first diagnosed when Kathleen was two. Her father's life insurance policy and a settlement from the other driver's insurance company had been the only things that had saved Kathleen and her mother from a life of desperation.

"Did you zone out on me again?" Raina asked.

Kathleen tore her gaze from her father's photo. "Whoops—sorry about that. So what's up?"

"After I dropped Holly at her house, I went

back to the hospital and found my mom and filled her in on our morning. I mentioned Carson Kiefer and she just rolled her eyes. Seems he's some kind of a problem for his parents. Nothing major, but he's got a rep for getting into trouble."

"I'm hardly surprised."

"Are you interested?"

Kathleen bristled. "No way."

"I just thought you'd like to know the buzz about him. Think of it as a background check."

"I'm sure our paths won't even cross. It's a big hospital."

"Maybe. Anyway, I also went to the volunteer office and picked up our polo shirts."

"How? I haven't turned in my paperwork yet."

"Mom arranged it. It helps to have an inside track. I also signed us up to start on Monday morning. Okay with you?"

"I guess."

"Good. Hunter and I have a date tonight, so we'll drop off your shirts on our way to the movie."

"I'll be looking for you."

Kathleen was loading the dishwasher that night when her mother, leading Raina and Hunter, rolled her wheelchair into the kitchen. "Your friends are here to see you."

"Shirt delivery," Raina said brightly, and dropped a bag onto the table.

Kathleen peeked into the bag. "Pink just isn't my best color. It's the red hair, I think."

"I got us each a blue one too."

Hunter grinned. "You two are funny. It's a volunteer job, not a fashion show."

"Kathleen's always fussed about her red hair, and I think it's just beautiful. Her father was a redhead, you know." Mary Ellen sounded wistful.

"How have you been feeling?" Hunter asked, quickly changing the subject.

Kathleen was grateful. She didn't want her mother getting nostalgic and depressed. The doctor had told Kathleen that some depression was caused by Mary Ellen's MS medications, but still Kathleen tried hard not to trigger any episodes.

"I'm doing all right. Kathleen takes good care of me."

"You look great. New hairstyle?" Hunter's compliment made Mary Ellen smile and reach up to smooth her hair. "My mom said for you to call her if you ever need anything from the store and Kathleen's not here. She'll be glad to run errands for you anytime."

"That's nice of her."

Raina took Hunter's hand. "Let's not be late."

"What are you going to see?" Kathleen asked, feeling envious. She'd love to be heading out to a movie with a guy of her dreams.

"Some dopey love story," Hunter said, with a wink.

"Better than some movie with a hundred car chases and flying bodies," Raina said.

"Since when? I like car chases."

"Go," Kathleen said, pointing to the door.

Raina said, "I'll pick you up at nine Monday morning."

Kathleen knew the announcement was for Mary Ellen's benefit. "I'll be ready."

Once they were gone, Kathleen turned back to the table and the bag. She shook out the two shirts, one pink, one navy blue, with the hospital's logo stamped in white over the pocket. On the pocket was an inch-high stylized angel sewn in white thread. She ran her finger over the emblem on one shirt.

Her mother looked up at her, her eyes full of tenderness. "The pink shirt will look fine on you. You're young and pretty and you look good in anything you wear."

"Thanks, Mom."

"That Hunter's a nice boy."

"That's what Raina says too. She says he's one in a million."

"You'll find a nice boy one day too. And you'll leave."

A warning bell rang in Kathleen's head. "Now, Mom, Prince Charming hasn't found me yet, and based on the guys I know at school, he won't be coming along anytime soon."

Mary Ellen sighed, backed up her chair and turned toward the doorway. "One of my shows is coming on TV. Want to watch it with me?"

"*No!*" Kathleen wanted to shout. The last thing she wanted to do was spend a boring evening watching boring reruns on the boring tube. But school was out, so she couldn't use homework as an excuse. "Sure," she said. "Let me finish up in here and I'll be in. I'll make us some popcorn."

"I'd like that," Mary Ellen said, rolling her wheelchair through the doorway.

Kathleen busied herself with making popcorn. Sometimes she felt totally trapped in her life. But what could she do about it? Her mother needed her. Through no fault of her own, her mother had a terrible disease and no one to take care of her except her daughter. Kathleen's father was dead and gone, and she would never have the chance to talk to him or have him as a part of her life. What had happened to their family wasn't fair. Not fair at all.

"What's on your mind, Raina?"

Raina had been staring into the depths of her postmovie bowl of ice cream. "I'm not being very good company tonight, am I?" They were sitting in a small ice cream parlor at the mall.

"You're fine company, but you haven't said much. The show wasn't that bad, was it? Not a car chase in it."

"The movie was fine. I just get depressed whenever I go to Kathleen's house. I feel so sorry for her. She really is a slave, you know. Her mother expects Kathleen to wait on her hand and foot. She has no life outside of school and home."

"And you think it's your job to fix things for her? Is that why you dragged her into the volunteer program at the hospital?"

Raina felt her hackles rise. "Is that what you think I did—fix things for her?"

"Yes," he answered without apology.

"If it was up to her mother, Kathleen would never leave that house. She needs a life."

"Listen, I'm not criticizing you. This is who you are and it's one of the things that makes me crazy about you."

She shook her head, instantly disarmed by Hunter's comeback. How could she growl at a guy who spoke with honesty but also with kindness? "I really think the program will be good for her. It'll help her think about something besides her duty to her mother."

"Like what—her duty to the volunteer program? What if she hates it?"

Raina flushed in exasperation. She saw his point: Was Kathleen just trading one duty for another? "Then she can quit."

"And you'd let her?"

"Well, of course. How could I stop her? I'm just trying to be her friend."

"And her mother is . . . ?" He left the sentence unfinished.

"Trying to lock her down," Raina finished with surety. "Holly thinks Kathleen's mother is suffocating her too—just ask her."

"My sister's so excited to be busy this summer that she'd have done anything you suggested. Kathleen's home life isn't even on her radar."

Raina didn't want to get into her feelings about Holly's life and how rigid and unbending she thought Hunter's parents were toward his sister. "Do you think it's a bad idea for Holly to volunteer?"

"It's a good idea. She needs to spread her wings."

Raina frowned. "And Kathleen doesn't? I don't get the difference."

Hunter shrugged. "I don't know how to explain it exactly, but there is a difference. Holly's trying hard to grow up. Kathleen's already way *too* grown up. Don't treat her like taffy."

"Meaning?"

"Don't pull too hard. Let her figure her life out for herself."

Raina tipped her chin. "And when you go off to college next year, Mr. Harrison, will you major in psychology? You seem to have sized up the lives of me and my friends like a pro."

He grinned self-consciously. "I like psychology. I like trying to decide what makes people tick and act the way they do."

"And what makes me tick? Have you figured that out yet?"

He braced his elbows on the table and leaned forward until their faces were just inches apart. "Here's what I know about you: You have a kind heart. You really care about your friends' lives. And you're sexy too. An unbeatable combo."

His bright green eyes made Raina's insides quiver. "Sexy? I didn't think you noticed stuff like that."

He touched his nose to hers in an Eskimo kiss. "Oh, I notice."

Her pulse quickened and she teased, "Isn't this place a little too public for kissing?"

"I pick public places on purpose. Private places are too dangerous."

"Why? Because of the Promise?" She brought up the thing that stood like a shadow between them. When he'd been in ninth grade, before she'd met him, and while attending a church camp, he'd taken a vow to remain chaste until he married. When she first started dating him, she'd respected him for that vow. It was a welcome change to date a guy who wasn't pressuring her to have sex, but now, after a year of dating, she would have given Hunter anything he asked for—except that he didn't ask.

He leaned back in his chair. "You know what they call guys who break their promise, don't you?"

"Yes . . . Daddy." She answered with the punch line to the old joke.

He gave her a thumbs-up. "Beautiful, sexy and smart. I'm a lucky guy."

I'm the lucky one, Raina thought. "Okay, lucky guy, can you come over tomorrow and hang by the pool with me? Once I become a Pink Angel, I won't have tons of free time."

"Tomorrow's Sunday."

"Oh, I forgot. Church."

"You could come with me."

She shook her head. "You know religion isn't my thing." She offered him a smile to soften her refusal. They'd had the same discussion many times. Hunter and his family were big churchgoers, but religion didn't appeal to Raina. How could God, who was supposed to be good, allow sickness and evil in the world? It made no sense to her. "How about after church?"

"Family time. My dad wants us together on Sundays."

She tried not to feel resentful. Her father had walked out on her and her mother when Raina was born, so Vicki St. James had been both mother and father to Raina. When she saw how Hunter's father bossed Holly around, it sometimes made her glad she didn't have a father. "Okay . . . no pool time tomorrow. What about Tuesday, since I'll be at the hospital most of Monday."

"If I don't land a job on Monday, I'll be over Tuesday."

"I thought you were cutting grass again this summer."

"On weekends, but I need a job that pays more money to help pay my way through college."

Her heart squeezed. Because soon he would be a senior, at the end of the upcoming school year he would graduate and while she was a senior stranded in high school, he would go away to college. She could hardly bear to think about it. A year without Hunter would be like a year without oxygen. "Holly told me that once you go, she's going to take over your old room and paint it purple."

"Over my dead body!"

Raina shrugged innocently. "This can be avoided if you go to the University of South Florida and live at home instead of heading off to Florida State, way far away from me."

"Are you blackmailing me?"

"No . . . just a friendly suggestion." She flashed him a sunny smile.

He took her hand. "Come on. I need to spend a few minutes alone with you in a private place after all."

"I thought you'd never ask," she kidded, following him out of the parlor.

In the car, he pulled her close and kissed her. She cuddled against him without speaking, knowing that if she ever told him how much she truly loved him, it might scare him off. And life without Hunter was something she never wanted to face.

four

KATHLEEN SPENT HER first two weeks as a volunteer in the admissions office filing paperwork and taking patients to their rooms in wheelchairs once they were admitted. Holly pulled duty delivering gift shop items, flowers and food trays, and garnered a coveted assignment as playroom helper on the pediatric floor. Raina prepared patients for transport to operating rooms or tests. She often ran errands for nurses and residents from floor to floor because she knew her way around so well.

As junior volunteers, they could work up to three days a week, reporting to the volunteer office on the first floor to check in and receive their assignments. From there they reported to the department head who had requested a volunteer, and worked until the task was finished or the department head no longer needed them. Then they would return to the volunteer office for another assignment, or go home if it was late in the day.

Kathleen liked the admissions office and wanted to remain working there. The work was easy, and she felt as if she were working in a regular office instead of a hospital. Her supervisor was delighted with her wheelchair skills, and when she asked Kathleen how she had acquired them, Kathleen only said, "I help out a sick woman in my neighborhood." Not the total truth, but not a lie either.

The only thing that gave her pause about the Pink Angels program happened on the first day she reported to the admissions office. She met a girl, Beverly, who was a year older and leaving the program. She was assigned to familiarize Kathleen with her duties. "Can I ask why you're leaving?" Kathleen inquired over the file drawers in the back room. "Don't you like it here?"

Beverly thought for a moment. "It wasn't what I'd expected it to be."

"What do you mean?"

"I became a volunteer because I wanted to help people. I thought this would be a good way to do that."

"It isn't?" Wasn't that why *she* had allowed Raina to talk her into joining—because she wanted to help?

"Let me tell you what happened to me. I volunteered last summer and liked it, so I stayed on to work after school and on weekends every now and again. Then last month, I was taking a patient up from the emergency room to be admitted when all you-know-what broke loose." Beverly paused, the stack of folders she was showing Kathleen how to file forgotten. "An EMS crew came running in, pushing a stretcher with this unconscious man. He was white as a sheet and one of the EMS guys was sitting across the guy's chest doing CPR. Another was holding IV bags. There was blood everywhere. I was pinned against a wall with my woman in a wheelchair and we couldn't move, so I had to watch.

"It was horrible. His leg was broken off and I saw his bone sticking out." Beverly shuddered. "I thought I was going to be sick."

Kathleen's stomach lurched at the girl's description.

"Anyway, I finally got my patient out of there, but I was totally shook up. Later, I went down, you know, just to check on the man, and . . . and . . ." Moisture formed in Beverly's eyes. "And he was dead."

Kathleen swallowed hard. "That's terrible."

"The ER was busy and so no one had come up to take him to the morgue, and he was just lying there. He looked asleep, but he was dead." Beverly swiped under her eyes and sniffed. "I tried to forget about it, but I couldn't. Every time I closed my eyes, I saw him. That's when it hit me. Hospitals help people live, but people die here too. I started getting scared that I'd see something like that again and I knew I couldn't take it. I asked Connie to put me someplace out of the way and this is it." She gestured at the room full of cabinets and computers. "It worked for a while, but now I just want to be a regular person. I'm not cut out to be a volunteer. So that's why I'm leaving."

Kathleen told Raina and Holly the story and although they were both sympathetic, neither wanted to reconsider her decision to join the program. "We'll never see anything like that," Raina said confidently.

"I agree," Holly said. "So far, it's been nothing but fun."

Kathleen wasn't so sure, but from that day forward, she asked to remain in admissions, and except for taking patients up to their rooms, or a pregnant woman to Labor and Delivery, she stayed off the upper floors and away from Emergency. She had a lunch break at noon and another break around three. She met Raina and Holly in the parking garage at five and rode home listening to Raina and Holly chatter about their experiences.

From time to time, Kathleen looked for Carson's name on the sign-up sheet in the volunteer office, but she never saw it. She told herself that odds were he didn't even think of her beyond that first day. Still, she wanted to see him again. He might have made her angry, but he *was* gorgeous and he *had* flirted with her. She kept the secret buried, even when Holly asked point-blank if Kathleen had ever talked to "the hunk from orientation."

"Too busy with my workload," she had said.

It was the middle of June. Kathleen was walking through an underground tunnel used to move quickly between buildings of the giant hospital when she heard someone call, "Wait up!"

She turned to see Carson jogging toward her. Her heartbeat accelerated, but she tried for an air of indifference.

"I thought that was you," he said, stopping in front of her. "It's Kathy, isn't it?"

"Kathleen," she corrected, feeling oddly let down. He didn't even remember her name.

He shrugged and tossed her a disarming smile. "Where you headed?"

"I'm delivering a file to a doctor in building two."

"I'm just starting the program today. Have you missed me?"

"I hadn't noticed you weren't working." She hoped he wouldn't see through her white lie.

"I'm wounded. Aren't you ever going to be nice to me?"

She felt color creep up her neck. "I—I didn't mean—"

"It's okay. How about we call a truce?" A lazy, sexy smile crossed Carson's lips.

"I'm not at war with you."

"Still, I'd like to start over."

Kathleen hugged the folder to her chest, wishing he didn't affect her the way he did. "Um—all right, where have you been?"

"I've been catching up on schoolwork."

"School's been out for weeks."

"Private tutor. It seems I skipped a few too many classes, and the headmaster was holding my grades and free pass to my junior year until I made up some tests."

Privileged, Kathleen thought. In her school, he probably would have flunked. "Glad you made it," she said, hoping she didn't sound cynical.

He bowed from the waist. Straightening, he asked, "Where did Connie assign you?"

"I've been in the admissions office since my first day. How about you?"

"I'm stuck with files and paperwork in my parents' office." He leaned forward and in a mock whisper added, "I think they want to keep tabs on me for a while. You know, before turning me out on the general hospital population where I might do damage."

"I can't imagine why they'd want to keep tabs on you." The remark was out of her mouth before she thought about it. And it sounded sarcastic. She could have bitten her tongue.

Carson laughed. "I don't think you have a very good impression of me, Kathleen."

"I—I don't know you at all." She hugged the folder tighter.

"That's true. Maybe we should fix that."

Her mouth went dry and her heart thudded.

"Look, I'm having a party at my place Saturday night. It's my birthday party, but no presents. A lot of my friends will be there. There'll be food, pool water—all the trimmings." He grinned. "Why don't you come?"

"I don't think—"

"I saw you with two girls at orientation . . ."

"Raina and Holly," she supplied.

"Bring them too."

"Raina's got a boyfriend."

"He's welcome to come."

She wasn't sure she wanted to mingle with kids she didn't know. Her mouth was so dry that she didn't trust her voice not to crack, so she simply nodded.

Carson reached into his pocket and pulled out a scrap of paper and the stub of a pencil. "Here's my address. Come around eight." He wrote quickly, jammed the paper into her hand, which was still locked around the folder and turned and jogged back through the tunnel the way he'd come.

By the time Kathleen found her voice, he had disappeared through a set of double doors. "I'll have to see if my friends can come with me," she said into the empty air. "I won't come unless they do. And there's no way I'm wearing a bathing suit," she added under her breath. She looked down at the piece of paper and at Carson's address on Davis Island, one of Tampa's most prestigious neighborhoods. She turned the paper over and saw that he'd written on the back of a week-old parking ticket. It figured.

"Whoa, missy. Where are you going?"

With her hand on the doorknob, Holly froze at the sound of her father's voice. She'd almost made it out of the house without his seeing her. She took a deep breath, pasted on a cheerful smile and turned. "To wait for Hunter on the front porch. He's driving me and Raina and Kathleen to a party. I told you about it at dinner last night. Remember?"

Mike Harrison scrutinized her. "You're not leaving the house dressed like *that*."

She glanced down at herself. "What's wrong with the way I'm dressed?"

"Your navel's hanging out and your top's too low. Your shorts are also too short."

"Dad, it's a pool party." She held up her bag. "My suit's in here."

"I don't care if it's a party on the Riviera. No daughter of mine is going out in public half naked."

"All my friends wear clothes like this and their parents never say anything! It's just fashion!" Her voice had risen.

"Thanks for the enlightenment, because I've never heard that argument before—'all my friends get to do it.' "

Holly clenched her teeth, willing Hunter to come down the stairs and rescue her. Where was he, anyway? "I'll put on my suit as soon as I get to the party."

"Let me see your suit."

Too late she realized she'd backed herself into a corner. She'd packed a bikini, a suit he didn't even know she owned, instead of her one-piece tank suit. "It's a new one," she hedged.

He took the bag, opened it and extracted a tiny white string bikini. His face went livid. "You're grounded, Holly."

"But Dad—"

"Go to your room."

"I—I'll get my other suit."

"Too late. If you don't have sense enough to pick the right suit the first time, how can I trust you to pick another?"

"I only own one other suit!"

"But you picked this one to wear. Where's your sense of modesty? You told me that you've never met these kids before. What are you trying to prove?"

She stamped her foot. "I'm not trying to prove anything. I'm modest. I know how to act. I'm not going to embarrass you and Mom, if that's what you're thinking."

"This discussion is over. Your room." He jerked his thumb toward the staircase.

Hot tears brimmed in Holly's eyes and she wanted to explode. He'd made her feel like a scolded puppy, yet she knew from past experience that the conversation was indeed over. She scrambled up the stairs, almost knocking Hunter over at the top.

"What's wrong?" he asked, grabbing her arm.

"Dad won't let me go!" she cried. "And why weren't you ready ten minutes ago? It's all your fault." She ran to her room and slammed the door.

From the foyer, her father shouted, "There go your TV privileges! You don't act that way in this house, you hear me?"

Holly jerked all the linen off her bed, wadded it and tossed it on the floor. Then she threw herself onto the bed, kicked her feet and wept. She heard voices below, and minutes later Hunter knocked on her door. "Go away!"

He came in uninvited and eased onto her bed. "Hey, don't cry. It's not worth it. I argued your case. I told him I'd keep a close watch on you, but he wouldn't change his mind."

"I really want to go," she said between sobs. "I hate him."

"Come on, you don't mean that."

She sat up and turned on Hunter. "He's a bully and sometimes I really do hate him. He makes me feel like I can't be trusted about *anything*."

"Look, he rode me hard too when I was twelve and thirteen."

"But I'm *fifteen*."

"Barely fifteen," Hunter corrected.

Her birthday had come in mid-May. Holly had skipped third grade and was always the youngest of her friends. And at home, she was the baby. "When's he ever going to let up on me? I'll never be old enough to do anything if he had his way."

Hunter punched her shoulder playfully. "I'll bring you some birthday cake."

"I don't want any stupid cake. I want to *go*. These are kids from Bryce! It's the coolest school in the city."

"I've heard they're a bunch of snobs. I'm only going because Raina's making me. And she's only going because Kathleen's making her. We probably won't even stay that long."

Holly sniffed, staring down at her hands. "Go," she said. "Tell Raina and Kathleen to call me first thing in the morning." He squeezed her shoulder and stood. "*First thing,*" she repeated. "Before we have to go to church."

He snapped his heels together and saluted. "Will do."

When he was gone, she cried some more.

* * *

Holly moped around her room until her mother, Evelyn, knocked on the door and came inside. She'd been out walking the dog when the explosion between Holly and her father had occurred. "What happened to your bed?"

"I decided to change my linen." Holly stepped around the balled-up sheets and crossed over to her closet.

Behind her, she heard her mother sigh. "It isn't very mature to wreck your room."

"But I didn't make any noise. I wanted to throw books at the wall."

"Wise decision not to," her mother said.

Holly whirled. "Why does he treat me like a baby?" She didn't really want an answer, because she knew her mother would side with her father. She always did.

"And why do you provoke him? What did you expect him to say when you went downstairs dressed that way? And the bikini . . . when did you buy it? I would have never approved that sale."

"It's just a bathing suit, and I spent my babysitting money."

"No, it isn't just a bathing suit. It's indecent exposure. Use your head, Holly. *Think* before you act."

"The two of you smother me," Holly said in exasperation. "How can I ever grow up if you won't let me do anything, go anywhere? Hunter gets to do whatever he wants!"

"He'll be seventeen in September, and a senior."

"And he's your and Dad's *favorite*."

Evelyn blew air through her lips. "We love you both just the same. Sometimes I wonder how two such different children could have come out of the same union." She gestured to the mess on Holly's floor. "Clean this up now." At the door, she said, "You know, you're lucky to have a father who cares about you. Look at poor Kathleen and Raina. I'll bet they'd love to have fathers."

To Holly's way of thinking, both her friends got along fine without a father to bark orders at them. She bit her tongue to keep from saying so while she waited patiently for her mother's lecture to end.

Her mother opened the door, but before leaving she said, "And as a reminder, tomorrow's Father's Day. Surely you spent some of your babysitting money on a card, didn't you?"

She left, and Holly stared at the closed door in silence. Of course, she'd forgotten. Now, on top of being furious with her dad, she had to make him a card claiming how much she cared about him. She sagged onto the bed. "I was probably switched at birth in the hospital nursery," she said miserably. One of God's little jokes.

five

"Geez, look at all the cars." Kathleen chewed her lower lip nervously. She was sitting in the backseat of Hunter's car gaping at the expansive lawn and driveway of the Davis Island address Carson had given her. The huge Mediterranean-style house rose three stories and was lit up like a Christmas tree. Cars were strewn up and down the street, parked haphazardly on the grassy lawn and packed bumper to bumper on the brick driveway. "Maybe we should just forget about it. It's already nine-fifteen," she said, looking at the dashboard clock.

"Why?" Raina asked from the front seat. "Okay, so I wasn't crazy about coming, but now that we're here, we might as well go in."

"Why not?" Hunter asked. "I smell grilled burgers."

Kathleen couldn't begin to tell her friends how scared she was about attending this party. Especially now that Holly wasn't with them. Raina and Hunter had each other, and Kathleen had nobody to hang with now that Holly had blown her chance to come. "Can we leave whenever if I say so?"

"Your call," Hunter said.

All Kathleen wanted to do at the moment was split, despite her making a case to her mother about coming. Mary Ellen had been anxious about Kathleen going out. And whenever Mary Ellen became anxious, she became clingy. "Who are these kids? Why do you have to go? You've been gone a lot this week."

"It's just a party, Mom. I won't stay late."

Kathleen had tried to anticipate her mother's every need before leaving. She'd made dinner and cleaned up, rented two movies for her mother to watch, prepared popcorn and made certain that the bed was turned down and ready.

"What if I get sick?" Mary Ellen had asked just as Hunter and Raina pulled into the driveway.

"My cell phone's on and fully charged. I left you a dish of Jell-o in the fridge—lime, your favorite. Now, enjoy those movies and I'll be home before you know it." She hustled out the door before her mother could think of another excuse to make her stay.

Hunter wedged his car against the back bumper of the last one parked in the driveway so that it straddled the sidewalk, barely off the street. He opened the car door for Raina and held the seat forward so that Kathleen could climb out of the back. "Come on. Let's go check out this party."

Kathleen followed Hunter and Raina along the driveway, where small, hand-lettered signs reading PARTY CENTRAL had been poked into the ground to point the way around the side of the house and to a tall privacy fence with a gate. Loud music, the babble of many voices and the sounds of splashing water filled the night. Hunter opened the gate and stepped aside. Kathleen saw a spacious yard and patio surrounding an Olympic-size pool sparkling with underwater lights. Large crowds of kids swarmed in and around the pool, their bodies wet and sleek. Kathleen and her friends' entrance was hardly noticed.

Kathleen immediately looked for Carson.

"Food alert," Hunter said, starting toward an expansive brick patio and the largest outdoor grill Kathleen had ever seen. Teak furniture littered with plastic plates and soda cans sat under an awning. A keg of beer stood atop one table along with a stack of plastic drinking cups.

"Let's grab a burger," Hunter said. "I'm starved." He'd had to work late and had missed supper.

"You're always starved," Raina said.

They wove their way to the grill, receiving a few curious glances along the way but no greetings from the kids of Bryce Academy. Kathleen wondered again why she'd come when she didn't know anyone except Carson. Unlike Holly, she wasn't interested in expanding her circle of friends, especially ones from Bryce, the snob school.

At the grill, Hunter grabbed a plate from a nearby table and started fixing two hamburger buns for himself. "Food looks good. Don't you want something?"

"Not now." Kathleen was afraid she'd gag if she ate.

Raina picked up a plate and a handful of chips.

"Well, look who's here!" Carson's voice cut through the noise level, and before Kathleen knew it, he was standing in front of her. He wore black swim trunks and a bright yellow tank shirt that showed off tanned, well-muscled arms. "I figured you'd gotten a better offer and decided not to show."

She ignored his dig and introduced her friends. Carson barely glanced at Hunter and Raina. He tossed his arm casually over Kathleen's shoulder and leaned forward. She smelled beer on his breath and stiffened.

"Whoops," he said, rocking back on his heels. "Where are my manners . . . Does the lady need a beer?"

"Just a soda," she said.

"I take it your parents aren't here," Hunter said, munching on chips from Raina's plate.

"Got called out on a hospital emergency," Carson said with a grin. "But if you're worried about no adult supervision, the caterers are in the kitchen."

"Will they supervise any food fights?" Kathleen asked.

Carson clucked. "You disapprove. Lighten up, it's my birthday."

"Happy birthday," she said.

"How about a birthday kiss? Your gift to me."

His eyes looked glassy. She ducked out from under his arm. "You said no presents, remember?"

"She always this way?" Carson asked Hunter and Raina.

"She knows when she's being respected or not," Raina said coolly.

He bowed slightly and said, "I didn't mean to disrespect you, Kathleen." She had no comeback, so she said nothing. In the next breath, he asked, "Where's your suit? Aren't you going swimming?"

"No," she said.

"But it's a pool party."

She glanced toward the pool, where swimmers swarmed like ants. In the shallow end, girls dressed in colorful bikinis sat on boys' shoulders and tried to swat one another off with large inflated tubes. Their squeals almost drowned out the blare of music from poolside speakers. Kathleen wondered if every girl at Bryce was thin and pretty, or if Carson only surrounded himself with the attractive ones. "Do you know all these people?" she asked.

"About half. It's a party and word gets around."

"What's this, Carson?"

The girl's question made Kathleen turn back toward Carson. She found herself facing the most stunningly beautiful female she'd ever seen off a movie screen.

Carson shot the girl an unreadable look. "Not a 'what,' Steffie. A 'who.' A person. This is my friend Kathleen from the hospital. Kathleen, meet Stephanie Marlow, an old friend."

Stephanie handed Carson a cup of beer, then draped herself around his shoulders. She was quite tall and her black hair was pulled back from her exquisite, fine-boned face graced with high cheekbones and set off by eyes the color of turquoise. Her bronze skin glowed in the light cast from scattered tiki lamps and candles. She wore a coral-colored bikini that showed off a flawless body. A diamond twinkled from her navel.

"Nice to meet you, Kathleen." Stephanie offered a smile that never reached her eyes. "But Carson has so many friends. It's hard to keep track of them all."

"Be nice, Steffie," Carson said, taking a gulp of beer.

"Aren't I always nice?" she said suggestively.

Kathleen had always considered Raina pretty, but beside Stephanie, Raina looked pale and colorless. And beside Kathleen, Stephanie Marlow was a goddess. Kathleen thought about saying, *"Nice to meet you too,"* but why lie? She also knew when a girl was staking out her territory.

"So you're stranded in that volunteer program like Carson? Were you naughty too? That's how Carson got stuck there, while I'm stuck with a long, boring summer without his company." Her perfect lips formed a pout.

"Not stranded," Kathleen said, hating Stephanie's condescending tone. "I *like* helping out. It makes me feel useful." And in that moment, she knew it was true. She became fiercely loyal to the entire program and every teen involved in it. And grateful to Raina for getting her involved, because she speculated that Stephanie had never gone out of her way to help anybody except herself.

Stephanie's frosty gaze raked over Kathleen. "Who does your hair? And your freckles . . . are they real?"

Kathleen's cheeks blazed. With uncanny accuracy, Stephanie had zeroed in on the part of herself that Kathleen felt most self-conscious about—her looks.

Carson untangled himself from Stephanie's

embrace. "Are her freckles real? What kind of a dumb-ass question is that?"

"Some girls paint them on," Stephanie replied innocently. Turning toward Kathleen, she explained, "I model, so I've seen it done a hundred times. Some girls think it makes them look cute and wholesome."

"I like her freckles," Carson said, weaving slightly. "Sure you don't want a beer?"

Raina intervened. "We were just leaving."

"So soon?" Stephanie asked without an ounce of regret in her voice.

"My boyfriend's on early shift tomorrow." Raina looked at Hunter for confirmation.

He had just stuffed the last of a burger in his mouth, but he nodded vigorously.

"Too bad," Stephanie said. "I was looking forward to making some new friends. Sometimes the crowd at Bryce bores me."

"Why don't you go inside and check on my birthday cake before Kathleen walks," Carson said, shoving his empty beer cup into Stephanie's hand.

Stephanie arched one of her perfectly shaped eyebrows at him, then called over her shoulder, "Hey, Denny, Steve, Russ . . . Carson's suit is bone-dry. You going to let him get away with that?"

Like overeager lapdogs, three large boys

rushed over from the side of the pool. "Steffie's right!" one of them shouted. "Let's fix it."

They grabbed Carson. He fought. "Cut it out! Lay off!" It only made them more determined. Carson was overpowered, taken to the side of the pool and heaved into the water like a sack of potatoes. He came up sputtering and cursing while everyone laughed and hooted.

"Come on. This could get ugly," Hunter said, grabbing Raina and Kathleen.

With the sounds of shrieks and splashes rising from the backyard, they hustled to the gate and across the lawn and piled into the car. Hunter backed out of the driveway and took off down the street. He slowed once he'd made the corner. Glancing in the rearview mirror at Kathleen, he said, "I had a feeling we'd all be in that pool, like it or not. Hope you didn't mind the quick exit."

Kathleen's heart was pounding and her hands were shaking from an adrenaline surge. Images of Stephanie and Carson bombarded her. There had been an electricity between them. Like a crackling fallen live wire, the current had run unchecked and dangerous. "I didn't mind."

"I'll bet the cops will show up too," Hunter added. "Parties like that are cop magnets."

Raina let out a screech of frustration. "They were a bunch of morons! Oh, and that Steffie. What a piece of work!"

"She was beautiful," Kathleen said quietly.

"She was a total b—" Eyeing Hunter, Raina stopped herself. "A witch," she amended.

He glanced at her and winked.

"Did *you* think she was pretty?" Raina asked.

"Is this one of those minefield questions like, 'Hunter, does this outfit make me look fat?' I refuse to answer."

"Coward," Raina growled, swatting his shoulder. She turned to look at Kathleen in the backseat, her expression growing serious. "Are you really interested in this guy, girlfriend? Because if you are . . ."

"Absolutely not!" Kathleen snapped. "He's self-centered, conceited and completely unreliable. He's a total jerk. I hope I never see him again."

"What about the volunteer program? You'll be running into him, won't you?"

"He won't last two more weeks," Kathleen predicted.

"Maybe," Raina said. "But for what it's worth, he does seem fixated on you."

Back at her house, Kathleen slipped quietly inside. All she wanted to do was go up to her room, but when she heard the TV in the den, she knew she'd have to speak to her mother. "Hey, Mom," she said, entering the room. "How are the flicks?"

Mary Ellen hit the remote's Pause button and

glanced at the mantel clock. "You didn't stay at your party very long."

"It was dull as dirt." Kathleen flopped on the chair beside the sofa, where her mother was stretched out.

Her mother smiled. "I'm not sorry you're home early. Even though I know you need to be with your friends sometimes, I was missing your company. I've only just started this movie, so we can watch it together."

"Works for me." Kathleen reached for the bowl of popcorn, now grown cold, on the coffee table.

"Tomorrow's Father's Day," her mother said absently. "They've been advertising it on TV. I wish Jim could still be with us."

"Me too, Mom." Kathleen felt a lump lodge in her throat. Not just for her dead father, but also for her mother, for herself and for all the things she wanted for her life but could never have.

six

On Thursday, Raina invited her friends over to her gated townhome community to soak up some sun by the community pool. "New suit?" Raina asked when Holly removed her cover-up and showed off her white bikini.

"I had to smuggle it out of the house, so please don't say a word to Hunter."

"Why not?"

"He might blab to Mom and Dad and I'll be grounded for life."

"Just for wearing a bikini? I don't get it."

"Neither do I," Holly said with a sigh. "If they had their way, I'd be wrapped up like a mummy."

Kathleen raised her head from where she was stretched out on a towel and looked Holly over. "The suit's cute." She was slathered in sunscreen because as a redhead, she didn't tan, she burned. "Hard to believe that it caused such an uproar last Saturday night."

"Tell me about it." Holly gauged the sun's angle and carefully laid her towel on the other side of Kathleen, then sat down and began to spread a film of tanning lotion on her arms, legs and pale white torso. "Do you know how bad I wanted to go to that party?"

"You didn't miss much," Kathleen said.

"Has Carson tracked you down since then?" Raina asked.

"No," Kathleen said. "But I didn't expect him to either." Privately, she felt disappointed in him, but also in herself. She had looked for him in the hospital halls when she transported patients but she hadn't seen him. Nor had she seen his name on the daily volunteer sign-up sheets. She wished she could figure out *why* she was attracted to him. She had a list of reasons why she shouldn't care, yet she did.

"He's probably in jail," Raina said, adjusting her sunglasses. "I'll bet his party turned into a free-for-all. And the beer keg probably didn't earn him points with anybody except the kids who were drinking it."

"I still wanted to go," Holly said. "You never know when a cute guy's going to come along and meet me."

Raina giggled. "You would have been dressed for it. I don't think I saw a girl there who wasn't wearing a bikini."

"Hunter told me about that Steffie girl."

Raina sat upright, a frown creasing her face. "What did he say about her?"

"He said it was like standing next to a pit viper. You couldn't be sure where she was going to strike."

Mollified, Raina lay back down. "True. There was definitely something going on between her and Carson. Don't you think so, Kathleen?"

"Yes, there was, but who cares? Can we change the subject, please? I'm tired of talking about people who don't matter one bit to our lives." She rolled over onto her stomach, but not before seeing Holly and Raina exchange knowing glances.

On Thursday, Kathleen got her mother into the van and drove to the hospital for a regular checkup with her neurologist and MS specialist, Dr. Emma Sanders. Since it was going to be a long day, Kathleen brought a book to read, but instead followed a technician when he took Mary Ellen down to Nuclear Medicine for an MRI. First Mary Ellen was given a special contrasting dye agent in an IV; then she was placed on a table that moved her through a tubelike machine. The machine took color images of her brain that would show lesions and help Dr. Sanders trace signs of changes in her illness.

Kathleen had begun reading about MS when she was ten and starting to understand that her mother was different from her friends' mothers. Her realization had come to a head when she was in fourth grade and a bratty older boy watched Mary Ellen's staggering gait in the grocery store and shouted, "What's wrong with your mother? Is she drunk?"

Kathleen shoved him straight into a display of cereal boxes and ran.

Kathleen knew the details of her mother's illness by heart: Multiple sclerosis is a disease that most often occurs in young adults, people in their prime. For unknown reasons, the myelin, the fatty tissue that protects the nerve fibers, is destroyed and replaced by scarring until the whole central nervous system—the brain and spinal cord—is affected. Over time, the victim experiences seizures, slurring of speech, vision problems and an unsteady walk, even paralysis. Yet there are long periods when the disorder seems to retreat and leave its victim in peace. Mary Ellen's flare-ups were unpredictable, and although she was on many medications to slow the progress of her disease, there was no cure.

When the MRI was finished, Kathleen and her mother returned to Dr. Sanders's office. While her mother was changing back into her street clothes, Dr. Sanders asked Kathleen, "How are *you* doing?"

"I'm fine. How's Mom doing?" These appointments made Kathleen nervous. She just wanted her mother to receive a good report.

Dr. Sanders stood, saying, "Let me show you something." At a light board hung on the wall, the doctor pointed to a clear, sharp MRI film of Mary Ellen's brain. "What do you see?"

Parts of the picture looked gray, speckled with dark patches. Others parts had bright patches, like sparks. Kathleen stared. "Mom's MS?"

Dr. Sanders nodded. "The bright patches are healthy myelin. The dark holes are where the tissue has been greatly damaged, even lost. Black holes mean permanent disabilities."

Kathleen felt her heart squeeze. "Is she getting worse?"

"Not necessarily. The new medications are helping, keeping her in remissions longer, I think. Time and future scans will tell."

"But that's good." Kathleen felt encouraged.

"Yes, that's good." Dr. Sanders flipped off the board's light switch. "Your mother's holding her own with the disease. But I'm thinking about *you* right now."

"Me? But why? I told you, I feel fine."

"You're her primary caregiver, aren't you?"

"Others help. We have a visiting nurse once a month and a housekeeper."

"But you manage the bulk of her day-to-day care, and you're only sixteen."

Kathleen felt her back go up. "So what? I can handle taking care of her. I've always taken care of her."

Dr. Sanders held up her hand. "And you do a great job. But who takes care of *you?*"

"I—I don't know what you mean."

"Do you plan to go to college?"

"Sure. My grades are good."

"Have you thought about where you'll go?"

"Maybe Florida State. My friend Raina's talked about going there, and we could room together—" Kathleen stopped herself midsentence as she was hit full force with an unspoken question: *Who would take care of my mother if I went away?* Why had she not thought of that before? She had wanted to attend college, with Raina, maybe Holly too. They'd talked about it, just the three of them, living together on campus for four years. Her cheeks flamed red and she looked away. "I can go to USF and live at home. It's no big deal."

Dr. Sanders said, "You know, we have a terrific MS support group here. The chapter affiliated with this hospital is one of the best . . . its members are very active and involved with one another. Has Mary Ellen ever attended a meeting?"

"While she was still working, before her MS got bad, she said she didn't have the time to spare. Now she says she doesn't want to be around a bunch of sick people. She thinks it would be discouraging."

"Just the opposite," the doctor said. "I try to

encourage her to go when she comes in for checkups. Maybe if you encourage her . . ." She let the sentence trail.

"I don't think she'll do it."

The doctor sighed. "It's for both your sakes, you know. She needs to get outside of her little world. And you need to have the freedom to live your own life."

"I do fine," Kathleen said defensively. "We have routines. I'm a volunteer at the hospital this summer," she added. This seemed to please Dr. Sanders, so Kathleen continued. "I didn't want to at first, but Raina dragged me, and now I'm glad. I like the work. I'm thinking about doing it in the fall, for school credit."

A knock on the door signaled that Mary Ellen was dressed and ready to leave. Kathleen turned to go, but Dr. Sanders caught her arm. "If you ever feel overwhelmed, come see me. Being a caregiver is not an easy task."

"She's my mother," Kathleen said.

"And you love her," the doctor said. "But remember this: Sometimes the best kind of love is in letting go. It isn't easy, but it's often necessary for the patient and the family alike. Not desertion," she added when Kathleen opened her mouth to protest. "But sometimes love must be tough. Try to get her to attend the MS support group. I promise you, it will be a help to both of you."

* * *

Holly's favorite volunteer job was any assignment on the pediatric floor. She loved being with the little kids, and it was soon obvious to everyone that they loved it when she came onto the floor. And it wasn't only the kids who liked her. The nurses and social workers did too, and the head of the department requested Holly frequently.

"I always wanted a kid sister," she confessed to one of the social workers when questioned about her aptitude for helping the little ones.

"Don't you have a brother?"

"Hunter, but he's older. I want someone I can bully around."

The social worker laughed. "Do you even know *how* to bully someone?"

Holly giggled. "I could learn."

In truth, she wanted a sibling so that she could be out of the family spotlight. If only her parents had another kid to "fix up" and make perfect, then perhaps she would have more freedom. She seemed to clash with them about one thing or another every few days. Her volunteer work at the hospital was the only thing she looked forward to and the only thing they agreed upon. Her parents gave high marks to volunteerism. In fact, her hospital volunteering was the only thing saving her from helping her mother with vacation Bible school and a long, boring week attending summer church camp.

"Camp's cool," Hunter told her.

They were doing KP duty one Sunday after dinner. Holly was putting away leftover food and Hunter was loading the dishwasher.

"Well, sure, if you want to bond with a bunch of girls," she countered. "Now, if it were a co-ed camp . . ."

"You'd get into trouble," Hunter said with a laugh.

"How do you stay out of trouble around here? What's your secret?"

"I keep a low profile."

"Very funny. And what about with Raina? How do you stay out of trouble with her?"

"I keep my mouth shut and bow and scrape a lot."

Holly slapped him playfully. "Not that kind of trouble. The other kind. You know. Just-the-two-of-you-alone-in-the-dark kind of trouble."

"We stay out of dark places."

"Don't you want to . . . you know . . . do the deed with her? I think she wants to with you." She had a momentary qualm about revealing what Raina had once told her and Kathleen in confidence.

"Too much information," Hunter said with a dip of his head and a reddening of his neck.

"You're embarrassed. I've embarrassed you! Cool." She grinned wickedly.

"Which is why Mom and Dad keep a lid on

you. What if some guy tumbled for you and got you alone in the dark? What would you do?"

She made a production of thinking it over before saying, "I'd jump his bones."

Hunter shook his head. "What am I going to do with you, little sister? Have some pride."

"Okay, okay, I'm kidding. I'd be sweet and pure, even in the dark."

Hunter studied her face. "It's serious, you know. You just don't give yourself away because some guy asks you to."

Holly got self-conscious. "I said I was kidding."

He resumed loading the dishwasher. "I love Raina. If . . . if we ever go that far, then I want it to be right. I'd want us to be married."

Holly sobered because she knew that Hunter wasn't kidding. He was dead serious and it wouldn't be fair to make light of his feelings. "Are you saying you're going to marry her?"

"Maybe someday." Hunter looked over at his sister and grinned. "But don't tell her. I want to surprise her."

"Ha!" Holly said. "Where are you living? That girl's already picked out her china pattern."

Hunter looked startled.

Holly burst out laughing. "Gotcha!"

He turned the kitchen sink's spray hose on her and she shrieked.

seven

"LISTEN UP. THERE'S going to be an ice cream social for Pediatrics, plus a fashion shoot over the July Fourth weekend." Raina read the notice aloud to Holly and Kathleen from the bulletin board in the volunteer office. "The hospital's asking for extra help. You two want to join me?"

"I'm on board," Holly said. She was putting on lipstick before going to her assignment.

"A fashion shoot?" Kathleen came closer to read the notice herself. "What's that about?"

"My mom said it's something one of the department stores does every now and again. They bring in models and photographers and do a fashion layout for the Trendsetter section of the paper. This shoot is for the fall season."

"But it's only July."

"Fashion and style work way far ahead."

"But the hospital—?"

"Some people think the hospital is cool,

Kathleen. The grounds are nice out by the little lake and the fountain and around the big banyan tree."

Kathleen had to admit that the tree was spectacular. Its branches were really part of its root system. They grew downward and once they touched the ground became part of the trunk. The tree had been on the grounds some fifty years and was quite a landmark.

Holly peered over Kathleen's shoulder. "Fall fashion . . . sounds like it would be fun to have a sneak preview. Might even be able to copy some of the new looks before school starts."

Raina patted Holly's head. "Our little fashion icon."

Holly had a gift for making anything seem fashionable. Every year before school started, she pored over teen magazines and copied the looks she fancied. Sometimes her parents forbade her to wear her creations out of the house, but her friends had to admit that she *was* stylish.

"I just had a terrible thought," Holly said, wrinkling her nose. "What if that nasty girl from Carson's party is one of the models?"

This had been Kathleen's first thought.

"What are the odds?" Raina said, dismissing the notion. She turned to Kathleen. "I've never seen Carson since his party, have you?"

"I haven't looked," Kathleen said, her face

turning red immediately. She'd always been a lousy liar.

Connie Vasquez came over to the bulletin board. "You three thinking about helping out at the social?"

"Sure, we'll sign up." Raina spoke for herself and her friends.

"Good. Holidays mean we run a leaner staff."

"Can I ask you something?" Raina didn't wait for an answer before plunging ahead. "Whatever happened to that Carson Kiefer guy? We never see his name on the sign-up sheets."

Kathleen could have cheerfully strangled her friend.

Connie shook her head. "That boy . . . he got into trouble concerning some party at his house. His parents hit the roof and sent him off to visit his grandparents. Evidently they live far from civilization, out on a farm in Tennessee, way out in the boonies. Why do you ask?"

Raina flashed an innocent smile. "We're just curious. So he won't be coming back?"

"I didn't say that. His father pressured Mark Powell to reinstate Carson into the program. Mark didn't really want to, but both Dr. Kiefers have clout here at the hospital and so he agreed so long as Carson isn't handling patient care. Frankly, just between us girls, I like the kid," Connie said. "He's intelligent, personable and downright charming. I just wish he could get his act together."

Raina wrote her name on the assignment sheet. "Well, I'm off."

Holly and Kathleen followed suit, although Kathleen shot daggers at Raina, who ignored her.

Connie said, "I wish I had others as loyal as you three. Many kids come into the program, but not everyone sticks with it the way you all have. We give out special recognition at the awards banquet in August." She grinned. "I'm talking real gold plastic here. All of you might have one in your futures."

The girls laughed. Raina and Holly walked toward the elevators and the upper floors. Kathleen headed off for the admissions office, where she felt safe and sheltered shuffling papers and working on computer files. Where she could do a quiet reality check about one Carson Kiefer—the guy she hated to like.

Raina met her mother, Vicki, in the hospital cafeteria that evening for dinner. "Sorry we have to have dinner this way," Vicki said as soon as they sat down with their food trays. "I have a ton of paperwork on my desk and I've got to catch up."

"No problem," Raina said, shuffling her food dishes off the tray. "I didn't want to eat alone at the house, and besides, this way I get to be with my favorite mother."

"Should I be flattered since I'm your *only* mother?"

Raina smiled. "Really, I like it here. Something's always happening."

"Now, don't you get sucked into this lifestyle."

"Why not? You like it . . . deep down. True?"

Vicki sighed. "Yes, I really love nursing. Except these days I've turned into a paper pusher. I get so sick of budget talks, staff shortages and scheduling dilemmas. I miss the good old days of actually taking care of patients. Which, if memory serves, is why I went into nursing in the first place."

Raina knew her mother's gripes were just because she was tired. She had worked hard and diligently to be where she was now—head of the nursing staff. "But you run the whole show. You're the boss."

"Sometimes it's more fun being a performer than the ringmaster."

"Are you telling me this place is a circus?"

"More like a zoo, I think." They laughed together. Vicki took a few bites before asking, "You like being a volunteer, don't you?"

"I *love* it." Raina laid down her fork. "Mom, I want to be a nurse too."

"After only a few weeks as a volunteer? It's a big world out there."

"This place is so . . . so *alive*. So exciting. I can't even think about going into some dull, boring job after I graduate."

"Believe me, this place has some boring aspects too. And you still have two years of high school."

"I thought you'd like the idea of me following in your footsteps."

"Sweetie, of course, I do. I think you'd be a wonderful nurse. I just want you to be happy. And these days, there are so many choices in the field. I'll help you check them out, if you'd like."

Placated, Raina resumed eating. "I'd like to know more about surgical nursing."

"Doctors have egos the size of the eastern time zone," her mother said over the rim of a coffee mug. "It takes a thick skin to be in an OR with some of them."

"You can't scare me. I've had Mr. Alvarez for math."

Their table was off in a corner, so Raina and her mother were alone. A few residents and interns drifted to a table in the center of the room. The cashier closed out her register and a janitor mopped the floor in a cordoned-off section. Vicki set down her mug. "And what about Hunter? What's he think about your ambitions?"

"He loves me no matter what."

"As he should. He's a nice young man." Vicki paused. "You two, um—" She searched for words. "I mean, you both *are* being careful, aren't you?"

Raina stared at her mother. "Did you just ask me what I think you did?"

Vicki lifted her hands as if to ward off Raina's shocked expression. "I'm not prying, Raina—honest. Just suggesting that you be careful. I wouldn't want to see all your dreams fall apart."

"You've already prepared me," Raina said, irritated. "Or have you forgotten?"

"Birth control is prudent and you know it."

"Hunter respects me."

"Oh, now, let's not fight," Vicki said, her tone conciliatory. "How many mothers and daughters can talk as frankly as we do? I'm sorry if I offended you, honey."

Raina glanced away, took a breath. Her mother was right. None of her friends had a mother like hers. Why should she get angry about a few questions on a topic they'd discussed off and on since Raina had turned twelve? She hadn't meant to get defensive. "It's okay."

Vicki reached across the table and took her daughter's hand. "I love you more than you can imagine, Raina. I want you to have everything *you* want without any roadblocks or glitches."

Raina cut her eyes sideways. "Do you love me better than chocolate?" This was something her mother had often said to her when she was a little girl and upset.

"Better than chocolate?" Vicki feigned shock. "Well, maybe better than chocolate pudding, but I don't know about chocolate kisses. I really love chocolate kisses."

They exchanged smiles. Her mother truly was special, Raina thought. In sixteen years, Vicki had overcome desertion by Raina's father, raised Raina alone *and* managed to rise to the top of her profession, making a good income. Vicki St. James was a winner. Raina only hoped she could be as successful once she stepped out into the world.

Kathleen was walking to the parking garage after her shift when she heard a horn honk and a voice call her name. She spun and stepped aside as a sleek silver Mercedes convertible stopped alongside her. Carson lifted his sunglasses and grinned. "Can I give you a ride?"

Her heart beat crazily at the sight of him. His black hair was windswept, his tan had deepened, and his dark eyes shone. He looked . . . well, *delicious*. Her gaze swept over the shiny car.

"My father's," he said, almost apologetically. "I drive a PT Cruiser, but it's getting new tires today, so I'm stuck with Dad's. Gaudy, huh?" He grinned. "So where are you going?"

"I'm on my way to Raina's car. She's parked on level three."

"Come on and get in. I'll drive you home."

She glanced around, hoping her friends might magically appear but knowing that she usually beat them to the parked car. "Raina takes me home every day." Kathleen shifted nervously.

"Leave a note on her car. Tell her I'm taking you home."

"I—I can't."

He pulled the car into an empty spot, got out, leaned against the door and looked her over with audacity. "Well, then, talk to me until they show."

She came closer, smoothed her hair self-consciously. Why hadn't she brushed out the frizz before leaving the admissions office? "How have you been?" she asked.

"Bored stupid. I've been in exile at my grandparents'. Have you missed me?"

Say something cute. Say something clever, she told herself. "I thought you'd quit the program." She grimaced at her lack of originality.

"I can't quit. You're here."

She gave him a level look. "Good one."

"You don't believe me?" He crossed his arms over his chest. "Really, I came back so I could see you again."

"Do you give these lines to every girl you meet? Or did you single me out?"

He threw up his hands. "I give up. What does it take to get you to accept me?"

"Honesty," she said softly.

His gaze shifted from flirtatious to serious. "Fair enough. I honestly want to know you better, Kathleen."

"And what about Stephanie?" She had to ask because she couldn't get the image of the two of them out of her head.

He braced his hands behind him on the car door. "I owe you an apology about her. She was rude to you and I'm sorry."

"She was rude to you too," Kathleen said, remembering how he'd been tossed into the pool at Stephanie's bidding.

"Our families are friends, and I've known her most of my life. She's kind of mixed up. Sometimes I feel sorry for her. Sometimes I could choke her." He grinned. "Not literally. I don't want you to think I smack girls around. She's a little crazy, so I cut her some slack."

"All right . . . I guess nobody can control the way someone else acts."

"You sure you won't let me drive you home?"

"Not today. But thanks anyway."

He straightened. "Well, then, how 'bout I take you out Saturday night?"

Her heart skipped a beat. *A date.* He was asking her on a *date.* "I—I don't know . . ."

"It's a yes-or-no question, Kathleen," he said. His eyes were so intense that she felt they were boring holes in her. Color rose to her face and she felt hot all over. "Yes," she mumbled.

A grin broke out across his face. "I'm sort of on restriction, so if it's okay with you, we'll go to the country club on the island for dinner. Seven o'clock all right?"

"Fine."

He got back in the car. "I'll pick you up at six-thirty."

"Don't you need my address?" she asked as he started the engine and backed out.

He looked up at her, a wry smile lighting his eyes. "I know where you live."

"But I never—"

He revved the engine and took off with a wave of his hand.

eight

"I'm doomed. I have nothing to wear and no money to buy anything," Kathleen said as she fell backward onto her bed, her arms spread wide in resignation.

"Don't be pessimistic," Holly told her. "We'll come up with something."

"Are you sure you want to go out with him?" Raina asked. She was sitting cross-legged on the floor of Kathleen's room, nibbling popcorn from a bowl.

Kathleen raised up on her elbows. "Yes, I want to go."

"All you've ever said is that you don't want to be around Carson. Then he corners you in a parking garage and you tumble."

"So sue me."

"Would you two stop it?" Holly said. "I'm trying to *create*." She began shoving aside hangers in Kathleen's closet. "Geez, Kathleen, don't you own anything except jeans?"

"I like jeans."

"I count ten pair. Where are your dresses?"

"In the very back, but they're all older than dirt."

"Can't you hit your mom up for something new?"

"No, I can't." Kathleen wasn't about to tack on the cost of a new dress to the already strained budget she and her mother maintained.

"We can go thrifting. Lots of garage sales in the paper for this Saturday."

"Hel-*lo*, Holly. The date's this Saturday night. I can't wait until Saturday morning to find something to wear. And what if I can't find anything?" Kathleen flopped back onto the bed. "I'm doomed. I'll find him tomorrow and cancel."

Holly and Raina exchanged glances. Holly said, "Raina, how about that green sundress you bought last week? You're both the same size."

Raina flipped a piece of popcorn at Kathleen. "You want to try it on? I'll bring it over tonight."

"Your *new* dress? You haven't worn it once. I—I can't wear it first," Kathleen protested.

"Well, there are conditions," Raina said. While her friends waited for her to name her terms, Raina tossed another piece of popcorn into her mouth.

"What conditions?" Holly asked, tired of waiting.

"That from now on Kathleen is honest with

her best friends. That when one of us asks if she likes someone, she doesn't deny it if it's true."

Kathleen's face flared red. "I don't know if I like him. I don't know him well enough yet."

"He's been on your mind since that first day at orientation, but you blew us off every time we asked you about him. Why do you have to be so secretive about your feelings? It's not like either of us is going to post it in a chat room."

Kathleen saw the hurt look on Raina's face and felt guilty. She had been secretive. She hadn't wanted to share her silly crush with them. She thought back to sixth and seventh grades, when they would lie around and tell each other their innermost thoughts and desires. Of course, then their fantasies had been childish and simple, centering on movie stars and athletes. "I didn't want you to tease me," she mumbled.

"Why would we have teased you?" Raina asked.

"Because whenever Carson's name was even mentioned, everyone had some kind of warning for me about him."

"People were just making comments, not judgments against your feelings—which no one knew about in the first place."

"What would *you* have told me?"

"To follow your heart."

The two friends stared at each other and Kathleen saw sincerity in Raina's eyes. She said,

"I didn't mean to cut my friends out. I'll be more open in the future."

Holly, who had been watching the exchange, cleared her throat. "Are we finished making up? Because if so, we need to get going on this dress project."

Kathleen and Raina burst out laughing at the petulant expression on Holly's face. "I'll bring the dress over after supper," Raina said.

"Pick me up before you come," Holly demanded.

"Well, of course," Raina said.

Kathleen hugged them both and walked them to the front door. She had just closed it when she heard the electric whir of her mother's wheelchair come up behind her. "What's up?" Mary Ellen asked. "The three of you have been hiding in your room for hours."

It had been hardly an hour, but Kathleen didn't correct Mary Ellen. "I, um, have a date this Saturday night, and we were deciding what I should wear." Kathleen held her breath, waiting for her mother's reaction to the news.

"Oh. Who is he?"

"His name is Carson and he's taking me to his parents' country club for dinner. I met him in the volunteer program."

"A country club. He sounds wealthy."

"I don't care about that."

"Is he nice?"

"He's nice to me."

"Because that's important, you know. A boy should treat you nice."

Kathleen could tell by the rigid way her mother was holding herself that she wasn't thrilled with the idea of Kathleen's dating. "Raina's coming by later with a dress for me to try on, and Saturday night, Holly's doing my hair."

"I used to do your hair."

"Not since I was ten, Mom."

"So what will you wear?"

"Raina's loaning me a dress."

Mary Ellen considered that and finally said, "I'm sorry I can't buy you a new one."

"I don't need a new dress, Mom. I'm borrowing Raina's."

"I just wish . . ." Mary Ellen left the sentence unfinished. "You won't stay out too late, will you?"

"Of course not."

"He won't drive like a maniac, will he?"

"He's a safe driver."

"You watch your beverage glass. I see on TV about boys who slip drugs into their dates' glasses."

"Mom! It's just a simple date, not a kidnapping. You watch too much television."

Mary Ellen looked stricken, and Kathleen regretted her outburst. "I'll make sure your dinner's ready before I go."

"I think I can heat a frozen dinner without your supervision. I'm not helpless."

This was her mother's way of laying guilt on her—her way of saying, "*I'm fine. I don't need you,*" when they both knew she did.

"Then I'll go start dinner for tonight."

"I'm not hungry," Mary Ellen said. She backed up her wheelchair and returned to the family room and her TV schedule.

"You look fab," Holly said. She was standing behind Kathleen in the bathroom with a can of hair spray and a brush.

Kathleen had to admit that Holly's magic fingers had done wonders with her mane of curly red hair. Partly up and clipped with a sparkly butterfly ornament, her hair framed her face in a nest of soft curls and tendrils. "Thanks," she said, unable to think of a way to express more gratitude to her friend.

Holly grinned and curtsied.

Back in her bedroom, Raina finished pressing the sundress and handed it to Kathleen. "Great hair, Holly. How's our time?"

"Fifteen minutes," Kathleen said, stepping into the dress, still warm from the iron. She was a bundle of nerves.

Raina insisted that Kathleen dab green eye shadow on her eyelids and bronzer across her cheeks.

"Too many freckles," Kathleen said, hesitating.

"Do it," Raina said, then finished off the look with a bronze-toned lip gloss.

Kathleen slipped on a pair of sandals and turned for her two friends.

"Stunning," Raina said, and gave Holly a high five.

"Yes, and it only took two hours and three pairs of hands to get me this way," Kathleen said, but she was pleased by her image in the mirror. The deep green of the sundress set off her slender neck and square shoulders. She wished again that her skin wasn't covered with freckles, but then her friends weren't miracle workers.

"We're out of here," Raina said.

"Do we have to go? We could wait until he comes and see his reaction," Holly suggested.

Raina grabbed her purse and Holly's arm. "Carson doesn't need to see us hanging around."

"True. We want him to think that this look is natural instead of the project it was," Kathleen laughed.

"Have fun and call us first thing tomorrow!" Holly called as Raina hauled her out of the bedroom and down the hall to the front door. "Call tonight if it's not too late!" Holly was saying as the door shut behind her and Raina.

At the last minute, Kathleen grabbed a lightweight sweater to cover her bare shoulders and went downstairs. She found her mother in the den, sitting in her wheelchair and nervously fluffing sofa pillows. "What do you think, Mom?" She twirled.

"I think you're beautiful," Mary Ellen said after a long, lingering look. "He's a lucky boy."

Kathleen beamed. "I made you some vanilla pudding. And there's a new carton of ice cream too."

"I saw them." Mary Ellen kept staring at Kathleen. "I wish your father could see you."

"Me too, Mom."

Both of them might have teared up but the doorbell rang. Kathleen gave her mother a quick kiss goodbye. *Showtime.* She went into the foyer and took a deep breath, then pulled open the door to what she hoped would be a whole new chapter of her life.

"Did I tell you how pretty you look?"

Kathleen glanced up from the menu to Carson, sitting across the table from her. "You did. But there's no harm in hearing it again."

The ride across town to the country club had been accompanied by music from his CD player instead of conversation. When he asked about her mother, Kathleen told him briefly about Mary Ellen's MS and the loss of her father. "So do you mostly take care of her?" Carson asked.

"I do the day-to-day stuff, but she—we—have other help."

He had no more questions about Kathleen's home life, which relieved her. It was complicated and she didn't feel like going over the details with him. Not tonight. Dates rarely came her way. A junior boy had asked her to the Christmas dance last year, but once Kathleen heard that he and his girlfriend had split three days before the dance, she knew she was just a tool to make the old girlfriend jealous. It worked, because the boy had dropped Kathleen like a hot rock afterward. Raina dated. Kathleen and Holly looked on.

"Sorry we're stuck here instead of someplace fun," Carson said.

They were sitting on the patio of the club's dining room, which was lit by glass lamps and candles. Their table held fine china and good linen, a small vase of fresh flowers and a votive candle. Moonlight spilled over the terrace from above and bathed the golf course in the distance in a soft white sheen. A few diners at other tables were talking, and elevator-style music played in the background. She realized that the club might be boring for him, but it wasn't for her. Most of her friends started off their dating life with fast food and a movie. "I like it. Where else would we have gone?"

"Clubbing."

The city had three clubs for the teen crowd,

but a person had to be seventeen or older to get in, so Kathleen had never been inside one. "I'm not seventeen," she said.

"No problem. I'll get you an ID."

She felt immature. What should she say to that? The truth? That she'd be scared stupid to use a fake ID? She was rescued by a waiter who showed up to take their order. She scanned the menu quickly, realizing that although she'd looked it over once, she couldn't remember a single item offered. She ordered the dish at the top of the menu, hoping she'd like it.

Carson ordered and the waiter left. "Not everyone likes calamari," Carson said.

"Calamari?"

"Squid."

Kathleen straightened. Is that what she'd ordered? "Um . . . well, I thought I'd give it a try."

"If you don't like it, just order something else." His smile, etched in candlelight, sent a shiver through her.

"It'll be fine," she mumbled, wondering if he was regretting asking her out. She didn't wonder long.

"Hello, Carson. I didn't expect to see you here tonight." The girl's voice caused Kathleen's insides to turn cold. She glanced over her shoulder to see that Stephanie Marlow had come up behind her chair.

nine

STEPHANIE STEPPED AROUND to the side of the table and Kathleen all but wilted as she was once again struck by the girl's beauty. Stephanie was dressed in something long and shimmery that clung to every curve of her lean, perfect body. Her black hair was pulled back in a sophisticated bun that nestled at the nape of her neck; her flawless face and smooth, silky skin glowed in the candlelight.

"Hey, Steffie." Carson rocked back in his chair. Kathleen tried to read his expression, wondering if he was pleased to see Stephanie, but his eyes held no clue for her. He said, "I thought you were out of town."

"Plans change." Stephanie was pointedly ignoring Kathleen.

"You remember Kathleen," Carson said.

Steffie's gaze cut to Kathleen, who hoped she could paste a pleasant expression on her face. "The little volunteer from the hospital? Yes, I remember her."

Kathleen felt as if she'd been slapped. *The little volunteer?* She opened her mouth to say something that might take Stephanie down a notch, but Stephanie had turned her attention back to Carson. "I was supposed to do a shoot in the Keys this week, but it was postponed because of the hurricane floundering around in the Caribbean. There's rain headed for Key West."

"Too bad," Carson said.

Kathleen was left to wonder what he thought was "too bad."

"Are you here with your parents?" he asked.

"Don't be silly. Dad's out of town on business and Mom's in South America." The tone of her voice sounded cold. "No, I'm just here with me."

Kathleen wondered if Stephanie always dressed so elegantly for dinner alone. Maybe she'd hoped to run into Carson.

"How about tennis tomorrow?" Stephanie asked.

"Do I look busy to you, Stef?" Carson nodded toward Kathleen.

Undaunted, Stephanie said, "Oh, I'm sorry. Do you play, Kathleen? I can find someone else and we can play doubles."

"I'm busy tomorrow," Kathleen said, not about to admit that she didn't play tennis.

"Maybe later in the week, then." Stephanie's cool gaze held Kathleen's, making her feel as insignificant as dust particles.

"And then I work as a volunteer." Kathleen emphasized the word *work*, hoping to make tennis seem frivolous by comparison.

The waiter appeared with their meals and set each on the table. Kathleen stared at the donut-shaped rings that must surely be her calamari and wanted to gag. Wouldn't that make Stephanie's day!

"I think you got mine," Carson said, and swapped his plate of buffalo wings for her fried squid. He looked up at Stephanie. "Can we talk about tennis some other time? We'd like to eat."

"Of course," Stephanie said with a shrug. "I'll call you. *Ciao.*"

She walked away, the heels of her strappy sandals clicking on the patio brick. Heads turned as she wove through the maze of tables. Kathleen sighed. "I don't think she likes me."

"Don't worry about it. Steffie doesn't like anybody."

"She likes you," Kathleen said quietly.

Carson's gaze zeroed in on Kathleen's face. "She's nice to me because we have a history."

Every cell in Kathleen's brain was screaming, *"What kind of history?"* but she didn't ask. Instead she said, "It was nice of you to change our plates, but I can take back my fried squid."

"You sure?"

"I'm broadening my horizons."

He exchanged their plates. She stabbed one

of the small rings and popped it into her mouth. It was firm and chewy but left a much better taste in her mouth than the conversation with Stephanie Marlow.

When they'd finished dinner, Carson drove Kathleen home. Disappointed because the date had ended so early, she exited the car as soon as he turned off the engine. What had she expected? He had taken her to dinner and now the date was over. End of story. "Wait up," he said, falling into step beside her. "I'll walk you to your door."

As they approached her front porch, she saw that her mother had "thoughtfully" left the light on for her. It seemed as bright as the noonday sun.

Carson stopped her just short of the porch and the shining light. Her heartbeat quickened. Was he going to kiss her? She wanted him to, but she was scared. She'd seen so many TV shows where the teens were coy and confident and knew just what to say and just how to kiss and be kissed. On TV, in their scripted worlds, kissing looked so smooth and easy. But she had precious little experience with kissing. It had happened to her maybe three times, twice during party games and once when a boy did it on a dare from another. Now, looking up at Carson's face in the moonlight, she knew he was no amateur.

"You're shivering," he said.

"Just a little," she lied. *Nerves*, she thought.

He repositioned the sweater on her shoulders, smoothed a tendril of her hair. "I would like to kiss you," he said. "But I'm not going to."

Shocked, she took a step away and said the first thing that popped into her mind. "Do you think I'll taste like calamari?"

He laughed and she felt so stupid that all she wanted to do was turn and run.

He pulled her close, rested his forehead against hers. "It's about anticipation," he said. "That's part of the dance."

"What dance?"

"The getting-to-know-you dance. You see, most of the time, people move too fast. And when you move too fast, you miss a lot."

His eyes were shrouded in shadow, and his breath felt warm on her cheek. Her knees went weak. "Slow's good."

He slid her sweater off one shoulder, bent and pressed his mouth to her bare skin. He ran his tongue along the ridge of her collarbone to the base of her throat.

Her insides turned to liquid and she closed her eyes, reveling in feelings of pure seduction.

"Delicious," he whispered. "I knew you would be." He brushed her earlobe with his mouth, then stepped away. "Until next time."

Her eyes opened and she fought to control

her breathing, her desire to throw her arms around him. She watched him walk to his car and drive off. She watched long after he was gone and the sounds of the night had settled around her. She stood just beyond the brightness of the porch light, her body trembling, abandoned in the moonlight, with only the faintest whisper of an evening breeze moving over her hair and body like a lover's hands.

"And he didn't *kiss you*, kiss you? What's up with *that*?" Holly sat on the floor of Kathleen's bedroom, disappointment dripping from her questions.

"It's called patience," Raina fired at Holly. "Will you get some of it, please?"

Kathleen was embarrassed. It was difficult to implement the new policy of telling her two best friends *everything*. At least she hadn't had to spill the details to her mother. Although Mary Ellen had looked at her expectantly when she'd come in the night before, and again at breakfast, Kathleen hadn't shared anything beyond "I had a good time."

Raina, sitting next to Holly on the floor, turned her attention back to Kathleen, lounging on the bed. "I'm glad he wasn't all over you—it shows respect. As for that Steffie, I'd have 'accidentally' knocked my water glass down the front of her."

"She probably would have melted," Holly said, making the others laugh. When they were younger, they'd watched *The Wizard of Oz* so many times together that they could quote every line.

"So now what?" Kathleen asked.

"You wait," Raina said. "Let him chase you."

"What if he doesn't?"

"He has so far. I doubt he'll stop this soon into the *dance*," Raina said.

Doubt nibbled at Kathleen. What could she offer him? When compared to Stephanie, who led a glamorous life as a model, she was pretty boring. Maybe Carson was just toying with her. If so, she swore she wasn't going to let him know how he affected her. How he left her weak-kneed and starry-eyed, like a silly twit. Nohow. No way.

"I wish someone would chase me," Holly grumbled.

Kathleen and Raina exchanged glances. With perfect timing, they pounced on Holly, who screeched and fell backward. Then they tickled her mercilessly, rolling around on the floor and squealing like small children.

"Must you go?" Raina was sitting on a swing in a vacant schoolyard and Hunter was standing in front of her, his hands wrapped around hers on the swing's chains. He had just gotten off work from the fast-food restaurant across the street and she'd driven there to see him before he went home. And he had just told her that he was going off on a ten-day mission project with the youth group of his church beginning the July 4th weekend.

"It's for a good cause, Raina. Our youth group is going to help build a youth center out in Arizona on a reservation. My minister called me personally and asked me to come. The time will pass like that." He snapped his fingers. "You'll hardly know I'm gone."

"Not true," she said, still feeling the keen edge of disappointment. She was missing him already.

"The kids have been raising money all year for this trip." His church had a large youth group.

"But why do *you* have to go?"

"They need the extra hands. Some of the kids who were signed up to go changed their minds. Plus Pastor Eckloes thinks I'm a good influence on the younger kids. Go figure." When she didn't smile, he lifted her chin and looked into her eyes. "You could come along."

"I'm already doing a volunteer job, remember? And what about your job? Won't you lose it if you take off for so long?"

"I've already asked the manager. He said it was okay, that he'd cover my shift. The job will be waiting when I get back."

"Are you still doing the camp counselor thing in August too?"

"It's my first time being a counselor and I promised. Plus I like the camp."

"Another week you'll be gone," she grumbled. "I thought we'd have almost the whole summer together. These trips spoil everything."

He slipped his arms around her and she laid her cheek against his shirt. "Think positive. Think of all the muscles I'll build swinging a hammer every day."

"I like you the way you are."

"All soft and flabby?"

Of course he was anything but soft and flabby. She could feel the hardness of his body through his clothing. She tightened her arms around his waist. But she knew his mind was made up and there was no use arguing about it. He was going. The aroma of deep-fried foods clung to the fabric of his shirt. "You smell like French fries," she said, trying to lighten the mood.

. He kissed the top of her head. "And you smell like summer flowers. Have I told you how much I love summer flowers?"

Raina went all soft inside. She pushed herself away and looked up at him. "How am I going to stay mad at you when you say things like that to me?"

"I don't want you to be mad at me. I want you to be happy."

"I know I'm being selfish. You like helping at your church the same way I like helping at the hospital. I'm sorry I was crabby."

"It's okay. And don't think for a minute that I won't miss you like crazy, because I will. I'll have a laptop with me and we can e-mail. Maybe I'll buy a few postcards and write you."

Raina gave him a reassuring smile and together they walked to the parking lot to go their separate ways in separate cars. In her heart, however, she felt resentful toward the minister who had asked to take him away.

Two days later, driving home from the hospital and after dropping Kathleen off, Raina shared her frustration with Holly. She finished her gripe with "I was already hating him going off to summer camp. I wish he wouldn't go on the missions trip. I mean, why? The youth group is huge. There are plenty of others who can put nails into boards."

"It's not just about nailing boards," Holly said. "It's the whole being-together-as-a-church-family thing."

"What do you mean?"

"Well, we don't just do this kind of stuff to help others—which is important, of course. We do it to serve God."

God was an abstract concept to Raina, religion an invention of men to find answers for the unexplainable. "Can't God serve himself? I mean if he's God and all . . . why does he even *need* people?"

Holly looked askance at her. "People are his hands here on earth."

Raina didn't roll her eyes, but she felt like doing so. "Sounds more like people are his puppets. I just don't get it." Holly's light brown eyes scanned Raina's profile, and Raina felt her friend's gaze as she drove. "What!" she said, irritated. "Do you have something to say?"

"It's hard to explain because it's all mixed in with faith. Faith, not slavery, motivates people to serve God. Faith is what makes Hunter tick. It's what drives him and makes him who he is."

To Raina, the implication was clear—because she had no faith, she could not possibly understand Hunter. That made her angry. She loved Hunter Harrison, and he loved her. In many ways, she was closer to Hunter than to any other person on earth! How could a silly thing like his church get between them? She dropped the topic because she and Holly wouldn't come to any agreement about their different opinions that day. Hunter was who he was; Raina was who she was. They had differences, but their love would bind them together forever. Of that, she was certain.

ten

"HOLLY, MAY I talk to you in my office?" Mrs. Graham was Holly's supervisor on the pediatric floor. Her request caught Holly completely off guard. She'd just signed on to the floor and was heading into the playroom for morning art therapy when Mrs. Graham stopped her.

"Now, or later?" Holly racked her brain to figure out what she might have done to earn a visit to the supervisor's office.

"Right now," Mrs. Graham said.

With a pounding heart, Holly followed Mrs. Graham into her tiny cubicle, where she shut the door and gestured to a chair. Mrs. Graham went behind a desk piled with papers and file folders. Seeing the messy desk helped Holly breathe easier. Mrs. Graham probably wanted her to file and straighten her work space.

"You like working with the little kids, don't you?"

"Yes. A lot." *No filing today,* Holly thought.

Mrs. Graham obviously had something else on her mind.

"I see that you've signed up to help with the July Fourth ice cream social." The party was only two days away.

"Yes. So have my two best friends."

Mrs. Graham steepled her fingers together. "Since I can't be there, I've been thinking of asking you to take on a special project at the party for me. I wouldn't ask if I didn't think you were the right person for the job."

"Whatever you want, I'll be glad to do."

"You have a choice about this project, Holly. You don't have to do it just because I ask. It goes beyond, shall we say, your regular duties."

Intrigued, Holly asked, "Um—what is it? Mop floors? Churn ice cream?"

Mrs. Graham smiled. "No, dear. It's a people project."

By now, curiosity was oozing out of Holly's pores. "Okay."

"I would like your help with a very special child."

"Special" usually meant difficult. Holly riffled mentally through the list of kids on the floor, and while some were cranky in their various stages of recovery, none of them seemed difficult to her. "Who?"

"His name is Ben Keller. He's just five years old. And he's in the cancer wing."

Holly sat up even straighter. "But I thought—"

"I know. We don't normally allow first-time volunteers to help in that area, but I've spoken to Connie and told her I thought you could deal with it. She also said you'd told her that you were planning to continue on as a Pink Angel after school started."

"I am." Holly nodded vigorously. "I love the program." Her original motive of working through the upcoming school year merely to avoid taking a science course wasn't important any longer.

"Let me tell you a little about Ben before you meet him." Mrs. Graham leaned back, looking more relaxed. "He was first diagnosed with a rare form of cancer when he was three. I was his nurse and let me tell you, he won my heart. He was in the hospital for four months before we achieved remission, and by then everyone on the floor had fallen in love with him. I mean, most patients don't stay here that long for treatments, but his circumstances were unusual."

Mrs. Graham shifted in her chair. "His family lives about two and a half hours east of Tampa in Crystal River. His father drives a semi and is on the road a lot. His mother is very sweet and very young. When Ben got his diagnosis, his mother stayed at the hospital almost round the clock and was here for most of his treatments. The staff sort of adopted Ben and his mother. It happens—you just get involved sometimes, even when you know you shouldn't.

"Anyway, it was a very hard time for his family, but his doctors finally got the results they were after and released him. The day Ben went home, we threw him a little going-away party. Cake, balloons, took up a collection too for a tricycle. He loved the one in the playroom."

Holly listened, seeing the scenes in her mind as Mrs. Graham described them. She felt very sorry already for the little boy she'd never met. "I guess his cancer didn't stay away, did it?" she asked, knowing the answer already.

"He was checked in over the weekend. It seems he's out of remission. And this time, his mother is in the middle of a difficult pregnancy and on bed rest. She can't stay with Ben. I went to see him. He's so sad. He just broke my heart. He remembered me, but two years have passed, and I have other duties." Mrs. Graham's eyes filled with tears, and so did Holly's.

Mrs. Graham cleared her throat. "Anyway, I thought of you and I thought how nice it would be if you could take him to that ice cream social and stay with him. You know, make him feel special and maybe not so alone."

"I'll go meet him right away," Holly said, jumping up.

Mrs. Graham grinned broadly. "I thought you'd agree. Introduce yourself to Sue at the desk through the double doors. Tell her who you are and she'll take you to Ben's room. And thank you, Holly."

"I'm glad to do it. Really." Holly's heart swelled with pride. Mrs. Graham trusted her and considered her mature enough to take Ben under her wing—more mature than her own parents considered her.

From the moment Holly stepped onto the cancer floor, she knew she was in a different world. For although the walls were bright, and every door was painted in primary colors and patients' artwork hung from the ceiling on fishing line, nothing could dispel the atmosphere of serious illness that hung in the air like an invisible mist. Holly walked straight to the desk and asked for Sue. A young woman said, "Peggy Graham told me you might come. Ben's in room sixteen. Follow me."

The room held two beds; one was empty. In the other, a small child lay curled in a ball, one arm strapped to a board so as not to dislodge his IV line and the other thrown around a large teddy bear dressed as a pirate. Sue said, "Ben, I want you to meet someone."

The child didn't stir, just looked straight

ahead, his expression the saddest Holly had ever seen.

"I'm Holly." Holly bent down so that her gaze could meet Ben's.

His lower lip quivered, but he refused to acknowledge her.

"He's been this way for two days," Sue said. "Stay for a while. Maybe he'll perk up."

Alone with the little boy, Holly found a chair and dragged it to the side of the bed. "I like your bear. Does he have a name?"

Ben remained mute.

Seeing a label sewn into the bear's fur, Holly leaned over and read: *Adam's Boo-Boo Bears, a nonprofit organization.* "Do you like pirates?" she asked.

Again, nothing from the child.

This was going to be harder than she'd thought. "Can I sit here with you?" she asked. "I'm really supposed to be helping other kids do art projects, but when they told me you might like some company, I wanted to come and meet you." No response. "Do you like to draw?" Nothing. She reached over and picked up a book from Ben's bedside table. "This is a *great* book. My dad used to read it to me when I was small. You know, before I learned to read. Would you like me to read it to you?"

Ben kept silent, but she saw his eyelids flicker. Encouraged, she took it as a yes. She flipped open the book and began to read him *The Cat in the Hat,* by Dr. Seuss. She read with passion, with inflection, with all the dramatic excitement she could muster. Ben lay still, never once acknowledging that he was listening.

When she was finished with the story, she closed the book, asking, "Did you like the story?"

Nothing.

"You know, I have tons of books at home." She was remembering the boxes of her picture books stashed away in the attic. "Why don't I bring some in and read them to you tomorrow?"

Silence.

"I'll take that as a yes," she said, standing. She touched his hair lightly and left the room. In the hall, she drooped, amazed at how much energy she'd used trying to get through to him. She had no idea whether she'd succeeded; she only knew she had thirty-six hours to bring him out from behind his wall of isolation.

"Poor little guy," Raina said after Holly told her friends about Ben during the ride home.

"He's scared," Kathleen said, matter-of-factly. Holly's story had taken her instantly back to her own childhood, to the day when the phone had rung and her babysitter had answered, then begun to cry. Kathleen saw with startling clarity the hospital ICU where she'd been taken to peer through a window at her mother on a bed, wrapped in bandages. She had not been allowed to see her father ever again.

There had been a funeral with a casket that she was told held her father. For a long time, she believed that he would come home, that the big box and the funeral had been a mistake. Her daddy would have *never* gone off and left her and her mother *forever*. But as her mother slowly recovered in the hospital, as she held on to Kathleen and wept time and again, Kathleen came to understand that he would not be back.

"Earth to Kathleen."

Raina's voice snapped Kathleen into the present. "Sorry," she said with a start.

"Where do you go when you check out that way?"

Kathleen shrugged. "Noplace. I was just thinking."

"We were asking whether or not Carson was coming to the ice cream event to help out," Raina said.

"He hasn't said," Kathleen answered. In truth, she hadn't heard a word from him since their dinner date, which left her to wonder why he hadn't called. What was so hard about picking up a phone and punching in a phone number?

By now, Raina's car was in Kathleen's driveway. Kathleen exited the car slowly, her emotions still stuck in a downward spiral of remorse and regret. Had she kissed her daddy goodbye that day? She couldn't remember. Had she done something to turn Carson off? She didn't know.

She leaned in through the car window and said to Holly, "I hope you get through to little Ben. If anyone can, you can."

"Well, thanks," Holly said, genuinely touched by Kathleen's sincerity. Sometimes it was difficult to keep step with Kathleen. She was mercurial—up one minute, down the next. *Still waters run deep*, her mother used to say. With Kathleen McKensie, Holly thought that was certainly true. Kathleen was as deep as the ocean, especially when she sat very still and got that faraway look in her eyes.

Ben wasn't responsive to Holly the next day either. She read three books and talked up a storm too. On the afternoon of the Fourth, an hour before the ice cream feast was to begin, she panicked and tried a new tack.

She breezed into his room and flopped into the chair dramatically. She furrowed her brow and looked directly into the little boy's face. "Ben, I have a problem."

He was sitting up, clutching his pirate bear, an untouched tray of food in front of him. He turned his head to look at Holly, which encouraged her.

"Did you know that there's going to be a big party downstairs and outside on the hospital's property today? They're having hot dogs and ice cream. There'll be some clowns and games too."

Ben looked at her but said nothing.

"My problem is"—Holly paused and glanced around, as if sharing a secret that was for him only—"I don't have a date." She blew air through her lips. "And my dad's sort of strict. You know, he's always wanting me to obey his rules." She added that part because she figured Ben would know about parental rules. "And one of his rules is that I can't go to parties alone."

Ben said nothing, but Holly could tell he was listening.

"So I was wondering if maybe we could go together. Just so my dad won't be mad at me." Nothing. "What do you think? You'd be doing me a *huge* favor. I really like hot dogs and ice cream. I'd hate to miss out. But if you really don't want to go, we'll stay here and I'll read to you."

Still, Ben simply stared at her. Her ploy was failing. "Okay, then," she said, reaching for a book. "I'll skip the party."

"I'll go."

Ben's voice was so small that Holly almost missed his answer. "You will? Oh, Ben, this just makes my day!" She rose. "Tell you what. Let me go find the duty nurse and we'll get you a wheelchair and head down. We're going to have lots of fun. Trust me."

He nodded solemnly.

"I really appreciate this, Ben. I *really* do." She ran from the room before he could change his mind.

eleven

"WOULD YOU LOOK at that! Those are five of the skinniest girls I've ever seen," Raina said, adjusting the eyepiece on her binoculars. "I could just gag."

"Will you stop, please? We're going to get into so much trouble." Kathleen kept glancing at the closed door of the doctors' lounge on the seventh floor, positive that they'd be caught spying at any minute.

"Lighten up. It's a holiday and no one's coming up here today." The suites of doctors' offices were closed for the Fourth, but Raina had sneaked herself and Kathleen up to the lounge that looked down on the hospital's lakeside area where the back-to-school photo shoot was taking place.

From this height, the people looked small and inconsequential, scurrying around the photographer's lights and light-reflecting screens like busy ants. A group of teenage models draped themselves over props brought in for the shoot— blackboards, student desks, bikes and a motorcycle. The site under the great banyan tree was supposed to be an outdoor classroom, but Kathleen thought the sets looked dumb. "We should probably go downstairs and help at the social," she said, glancing over her shoulder once more.

"Relax. We've got over an hour before the party starts."

Kathleen kept fidgeting. Why had she let Raina talk her into coming up here in the first place? *Because you wanted to see Stephanie without her seeing you.* She answered her own question immediately. Raina's mother had inadvertently alerted Raina as to Stephanie's participation in the shoot when Vicki had shared a routine memo about it. No one was allowed on hospital grounds without a security pass, so the memo listed the names of all people who'd be issued such passes on July Fourth. Stephanie's name leapt off the paper when Raina looked it over, and she'd grabbed Kathleen and dragged her and a pair of binoculars to the lounge for a look-see.

Raina pressed the binoculars to the window. "Yuck. If that's what's being worn in September, I'll be sticking to my old wardrobe."

Kathleen saw a trailer off to one side where the models disappeared from time to time to change outfits. "What's happening now?"

"On the other hand," Raina said, ignoring Kathleen's question, "you'll be right at home, girlfriend. Looks like denim is in, big-time."

"Are you still ragging on me about my jeans collection?"

"Course not. But now you must have a jeans jacket trimmed in faux fur."

"You're kidding." In Tampa, it was hot as blazes well into the fall.

"Whoa—look at the food on that table." Raina poked Kathleen with her elbow without lowering the binoculars. "And one of the models is chowing down. She'll probably be over in the bushes barfing in a few minutes, though." Raina snorted.

"That's a hateful thing to say." Kathleen tapped her foot with growing impatience, and finally, unable to contain her curiosity any longer, she grabbed the binoculars out of Raina's hands. "Give them to me." She parked the lenses in front of her eyes and the people came into such close-up focus that she almost jumped backward.

"Hey, don't break my nose," Raina said while rubbing it.

Kathleen ignored her and swung the binoculars back and forth, settling first on the photographer, who seemed to be barking orders, then over to the models, who looked bored. Her palms grew sweaty as she swept across the models' faces. The girls were all attractive. She focused on Stephanie. Her heart sank. While the other girls were attractive, Stephanie was beautiful. In full makeup, with her hair professionally styled for the shoot and the clothing fitting her body perfectly, she outdazzled the others like an exotic flower.

"What's up?" Raina asked.

"Stephanie," Kathleen said quietly. "How can I compete against someone who looks like her?"

Raina took Kathleen's shoulder and turned her till they stood face to face. Kathleen lowered the binoculars as Raina said, "Now, listen up. I don't know why you feel inferior to that girl. She's vain, shallow and probably has gotten everything she wants just because she's pretty."

"So what's your point?"

"*Pretty* doesn't make for *better*. I've met her, and you're head and shoulders above her in every way."

"That's nice of you to say, but we both know that pretty counts in life. Boys go after the pretty ones. I remember how they hit on you from sixth grade on. Until Hunter came along, that is," Kathleen added hastily.

Raina's expression went stony at the mention of the boyfriends who had preceded Hunter, and Kathleen regretted her words instantly. Still, it was the truth—boys had clustered around Raina like bees around a honeycomb. "Sorry. I only meant to say that boys like pretty girls and you're pretty, and you always have been."

"But it's *you* that Carson is coming after."

"Then why hasn't he called me?"

"Who knows why guys do anything? Why don't you call him?"

"I wouldn't know what to say to him."

"Wouldn't you think of something to say if he called you?"

"I—I guess."

"Then I rest my case. If he's not here today helping at the ice cream party, call him."

Kathleen said nothing but raised the binoculars and twirled the focus wheel toward the photo shoot. Without warning, Stephanie's face came into full view, filling up the lenses and looking for all the world as if she were staring straight into Kathleen's eyes. Kathleen gasped, jerked the binoculars away from her face, thrust them into Raina's hands and fled the room.

A number of canvas canopies had been set up in the hospital's garden area along the walkways on the south grounds. Under each stood tables for games and activities to amuse and entertain the pediatric patients. There were face painting, fortune-telling, magnetic fishing games, finger painting and plaster hand casting. One special canopy hung above picnic tables with brightly colored table cloths, a popcorn machine, a cotton candy machine, a slush maker and a large cooler holding tubs of ice cream.

"Some spread," Kathleen said as she and Raina pushed two kids in wheelchairs along the path.

"Mom said some grateful father is paying the bill this year," Raina told her. "She also told me that sometimes the Pink Angels have fund-raisers for these parties. They have a big one at Christmas. Can you imagine being stuck in the hospital over the holidays?"

"I guess we'll be helping at the Christmas party, then, won't we? I mean, since we're signing on for the extended program."

"You too?" Raina asked, surprised. "I wasn't sure you would. I mean, you really weren't that crazy about the idea when we started."

Kathleen shrugged. "I've changed my mind. The place grows on you and besides, it's a credit."

"Hey, wait up!" Holly called from behind them. Both girls turned to see her pushing a small boy in a wheelchair. "This is Ben," she said with a beaming smile. "He's my date this afternoon."

Ben had large, luminous blue eyes and a head of curly blond hair. Kathleen waved, but Ben looked away shyly. She introduced her wheel-chair patient, Darla, an eight-year-old girl with a compound ankle fracture set in a cast to her knee. Raina introduced Sally, a seven-year-old whose burned hands were wrapped in gauze.

"Your date, huh?" Raina said.

"It was the only way I could get him to come," Holly whispered to her friends.

"How about some face painting?" Raina asked.

Raina's and Kathleen's charges agreed enthusiastically. Ben remained quiet.

They went over to the tables and after parking the chairs, each girl grabbed a brush and a tray of watercolors. "What would you like me to paint?" Raina asked Darla.

"How about you, Ben?" Holly asked. "Anything special?" His little shoulders rose in a shrug. "How about a bear?"

"You can draw a bear?" Raina looked skeptical.

Holly grinned. "Decals. For the artistically challenged." She picked through an assortment on the table until she found a smiling bear cub.

But Darla wouldn't hear of such a shortcut. She wanted Kathleen to hand-paint a flower on her face. And so did Sally. The girls set to work. Kathleen was leaning close, concentrating on painting the flower's petals, when Darla said, "You sure have a lot of freckles."

Kathleen sighed. "I know. Sometimes I wish I didn't have so many."

Darla kept staring. After a time she said, "I like them."

"Really?"

"I like them too." Carson's voice so startled Kathleen, she almost dropped the brush. "Nice work," he said.

"I—I didn't know you were here."

"I'm dishing ice cream." He motioned toward

the cooler. "I do it every year. It's fun and the kids like it."

She wouldn't have expected it of him. He'd been invisible ever since their date and now suddenly, here he was, looking at her with his heart-stopping grin and sexy brown eyes. She would have liked to ignore him but couldn't. "How nice of you," she said coolly.

"I'm on a break right now. I saw you and figured I'd invite you over for an ice cream sundae. You *are* planning on eating ice cream, aren't you?"

"It's up to Darla."

Darla glanced between them. "Do you like each other?"

"I like her," Carson said. "Why do you ask?"

" 'Cause her face is all red."

Kathleen could have slid through her chair's slats. "I think I'm finished with your flower, Darla," she said crisply, setting the brush in a jar of water.

"Then I want ice cream," Darla said.

"Smart choice," Carson said, and winked.

"Don't you want to play some games first?" Kathleen asked.

"No, I want ice cream. But I want him to get it for me. I like chocolate with candy sprinkles."

"He's on break," Kathleen said.

"Break's over." Carson grinned down at Darla. "Your flower looks terrific."

Kathleen glanced at Raina and Holly, hoping they'd come with her. Raina said, "I'm still working on a masterpiece here."

"Me too," Holly said.

Kathleen almost shouted, *"How hard is it to put on a bear decal?"* but decided against it. "Okay," she said to Darla. "Ice cream it is."

They followed Carson, who went behind the cart to stand with another server while they got in line. He made a production out of creating their sundaes. Minutes later, the three of them were sitting at a table with their ice cream concoctions. "I thought you were working," Kathleen said, still feeling testy.

"Still on break. Do you mind if I sit with you?"

"I don't mind," Darla said, giving him a decidedly adoring look.

He didn't wait for Kathleen's vote.

While Carson and Darla chatted amiably about Darla's injury, Kathleen concentrated on her dish of ice cream. She also watched Darla's little face light up while she talked to Carson and realized that all females were susceptible to his charms, regardless of age. This was his gift—to wind girls around his little finger. Kathleen did a slow burn, disgusted with herself for falling for him.

She was thinking of ways to blow him off and

put him down when she heard "I'm finished. Are you?"

The question came from Stephanie, who had materialized behind Darla's chair, holding a clothing bag over one shoulder and a makeup kit in her hand.

Kathleen choked on a bite of ice cream and all thoughts of dissing Carson fled.

"Not yet," Carson told Stephanie, without even looking up.

With a jolt, Kathleen realized he'd been expecting her.

Stephanie said, "It's been a long day for me. When will you be ready?" As usual, Stephanie looked through Kathleen as if she were a pane of glass.

Carson turned to Kathleen. "I lost my car privileges for a week, so I caught a ride with Steffie today."

"And now Steffie's ready to go," Stephanie said.

"But I'm not. I'm here to help and I've got work to do."

"You don't look very busy."

"You can ride with me and my friends," Kathleen blurted out without thinking.

Carson considered the offer before asking, "Are you sure? I live out of your way."

"Absolutely." She wasn't sure at all and

realized that she'd just committed Raina's car to a trip across town. She didn't care. At the moment all that mattered was besting Stephanie.

Carson told Stephanie, "Go on without me."

Kathleen held her breath and watched Carson and Stephanie engage in a silent battle of wills. There was something between them, an undercurrent she'd felt before but couldn't read. In the end, Stephanie turned and walked away without another word.

"I'd better get busy." Carson stood and stretched as if nothing had happened. "Where should we meet?"

Kathleen's mind was racing. What was she going to say to Raina? "I'll meet you in the main lobby after we get all the kids back up to the floor."

"I'll be waiting." He gave Darla a smile and a light tug on a hank of her hair. "Nice to share ice cream with you. You get that ankle well, and no more skateboarding tricks."

"Bye, Carson." After Carson had returned to the cart, Darla looked at Kathleen. "Do you know that girl?"

"Sort of."

"She isn't very nice."

Kathleen suppressed a smile. She couldn't have agreed more.

twelve

THE SECOND KATHLEEN cornered Raina alone, she told her what she'd done. "I don't know what I was thinking. But there Stephanie stood, looking all smug and dictatorial, and it was obvious that Carson didn't want to go with her. Can we take him out to Davis Island? I'll pay for the gas."

Raina looked amused. "What am I going to do with you, girlfriend? Why don't you make up your mind about this guy? Do you want him or not?"

"It's not that easy. Not for me."

Raina looked sympathetic. "I don't blame you about wanting to best Stephanie, but *you* can drive him home."

"Me! Can't we all go together?"

"I want to get home because Hunter said he'd call. Holly said she was expected at a family cookout. Where is she, anyway?" Raina looked down the hallway. All the children had been tucked into their rooms and only a lone nurse could be seen in the corridor.

"She wanted to stay with Ben until he fell asleep."

"Poor little guy. Well, he's got a friend in our Holly, doesn't he?" Raina turned to face Kathleen. "Now, as I was saying, you can drop me and Holly at our houses, then drive Carson home in my car."

"You wouldn't mind?"

"Why should I mind? I'm alone and wishing I wasn't. Go have a good time."

"But your car—"

"Return it tomorrow."

It was a nonvolunteer day at the hospital. Kathleen said, "Thanks. A lot."

Raina caught Kathleen's arm. "Listen, don't let that nasty girl interfere with what you want. If you want this guy, make the most of this opportunity."

"I appreciate your advice, but then it might not be about what *I* want but about what *he* wants. You know?" Kathleen sighed. "I wish I had more experience with guys. Just remember, while the boys were following you around like trained puppies, I was wallpaper."

"Take it from me, popularity isn't all it's cracked up to be."

Kathleen had never been popular, so she couldn't argue. Besides, Raina was right—she should make the most of being alone with Carson tonight.

* * *

By the time Holly joined them and they'd shared the plan for the evening, Kathleen was certain that Carson had grown tired of waiting for her and had called a friend to come get him. However, when the three of them reached the main lobby, Kathleen saw him slouched on a sofa, staring at a ball game on the lobby's big-screen TV.

He popped up and joined Kathleen and her friends. "Glad you're here. The game stinks because the Marlins are losing."

By the time Raina handed the car keys over to Kathleen, dusk had given way to twilight. By the time they reached Carson's house, it would be completely dark.

Alone together in the car, Kathleen found herself at a loss for words. It had been easier with Holly and Raina to carry the conversation. "Um—you'll have to direct me to your house once we get on the island," she said.

"No problem." He turned on the radio and found a station he liked. When they rolled over the bridge to the island, he gave her directions. She recognized the grand home from the night of the party, except that now only a few lights shone through the lower-story windows. She stopped in the driveway, and he reached over and switched off the ignition before she could do it.

"I want you to come inside with me," he said. "I want to show you something."

She thought about having to meet his parents and felt her stomach tie in knots.

As if reading her mind, he said, "Don't worry, my folks are at a party."

Her hands went cold and clammy. "No one's home?"

"Are you afraid of me, Kathleen?"

Irritated, she snapped, "No way."

"Then come on." He led her along a walkway lined with accent lights and up the brick steps and unlocked the front door.

From the moment she stepped inside, Kathleen felt like a fish out of water. The night of the party, she'd not gone into the house, so she'd had no idea how truly magnificent his home was until this moment. The foyer was enormous, with limestone flooring and hand-painted Spanish tile. When Carson flipped on a wall switch, a wrought-iron chandelier gleamed with lights high above. In front of her, Kathleen saw a wide staircase with carpeted steps and ornate black iron handrails. "Nice place," she said, trying not to gawk.

"My mom had it built to look like a Spanish hacienda. Follow me." He held out his hand.

She went with him up the double staircase. Her heart hammered. "Where are we going?"

"I told you I want to show you something."

"What?" She pulled back at the top of the landing, suddenly wary.

"You'll like this. Trust me."

She didn't trust him or herself, but she went anyway. The upper floor was softly carpeted, lit by iron sconces along the walls. He stopped in front of a set of double doors and flipped a handle, and the door swung open to reveal a room lit only by one small desk lamp. "Where are we?"

"The library."

"Are you going to read me a book?"

"We're going to walk through to another set of doors and then go out onto the second-story balcony," he explained patiently.

They crossed the carpeted library and stepped onto a tiled balcony with a cozy arrangement of rattan furniture and miniature palms. The balcony overlooked the backyard, where the pool glistened. Still holding her hand, Carson picked up a remote from a side table and dimmed the pool lights with the push of a button. "My dad's a gizmo freak. Believe me, we have 'em all." He led her to a setee, where they sat, shoulders touching, his hand entwined in hers.

She longed to ask, *"Now what?"*

"Watch," he whispered in her ear, making gooseflesh prickle along her neck and arms. He pointed skyward.

Suddenly, the sky filled with fireworks. She was so startled that she jumped.

"It's July Fourth, remember," he said. "This is the best place in the world to watch the fireworks

that I know of. Practically a command perform-
ance."

Fireworks? He'd brought her here to watch
fireworks? Kathleen's temper went off like the explosions in the sky. "You could have said something! You could have asked me. You didn't have
to act so freaking mysterious!" She stalked to the
railing. He came to her side.

"I wanted to surprise you. I wanted you to
watch the fireworks with me."

"So why didn't you just *ask?*"

"You were quiet as a stone in the car. I got the
feeling that all you wanted to do was dump me
and run off. Like I was a chore you promised to
do."

His assessment wasn't far off the mark, which
bothered her, but what he didn't know was that
fear, not inconvenience, had motivated her.
"That's not true—"

He took her shoulders and turned her to face
him. "I've never met a girl like you. It's like
you're afraid of having a good time. Like you'll be
punished if you start having too much fun."

His evaluation shocked her. "I know how to
have fun! I had a good time on our date, but
when you didn't call—" She stopped herself, furious that she'd blurted out her frustration. She
hadn't wanted him to think she'd sat by the
phone waiting for it to ring.

"And I didn't want to crowd you. You seem

scared of me. Are you? I don't want you to be scared of me."

She was and she wasn't. She was mostly scared of her caring too much and of his not caring enough. "I keep wondering why you mess with me," she told him, her anger gone. "You know plenty of girls. Pretty girls," she added. *Like Stephanie*, she didn't say.

"You make me sound shallow, as if pretty is a measuring stick for determining what I want. That's not fair. And that's not me." His eyes had narrowed and there was an edge to his voice.

When he put it that way, it did sound shallow, but just as she'd told Raina earlier, that was what she assumed all boys wanted—pretty girls to drape themselves over in the halls and in the school parking lots and in the malls and every place in between. Pretty girls were a guy's ticket to cooldom.

"So what *do* you want?" Her heart was beating so fast, she could hear it in her ears.

"Look," he said, pointing skyward. Beautiful starbursts of color broke over the trees and fell like handfuls of glitter. "I want to feel like that inside myself whenever *my* girl comes walking toward me. And I want her to feel the same way about me."

Who didn't want to feel that way? Who didn't want one special somebody to care about? Her emotions tangled with her logic and somehow both got caught in Carson's eyes. Her fragile feelings, so long held in check, splintered like the explosions in the sky, showering her mind with sparkles of possibility. "And if that should happen . . . you know . . . that explosion thing . . . between us . . . ?" Her voice quivered.

"Then I guess we'll just have to ride the wave and see where we fall to earth."

A part of her brain wanted to say, *"But falls hurt. People break."* She saw his face, his lips, as if through a mist. He lifted her chin and his mouth was on hers, warm and soft, and as if by magic, the fireworks left the sky and entered her body and soul.

In the space of the next hour, Kathleen went from being a girl who had hardly ever been kissed to one who'd been kissed thoroughly. Carson kissed her until the fireworks ended, until the sky had gone dark and the humid tropical air left them both damp and sticky. He took her inside to the coolness of the library, to the sofa, and there he pressed her body to his and kissed her face, her throat, her neck and bare shoulders, until she was drenched with desire for him.

From far away, she heard a clock gong. "I need to go," she told him. What if his parents returned and found her with him?

"I know," he said, his voice husky.

Every inch of her seemed on fire when he put

her in the car. He leaned through the window and kissed her one last time. "I'll call you tomorrow."

She backed out of the driveway and made it to the stop sign at the corner before she saw her cell phone glowing on the console where she'd left it. Her eyes widened and her body, which had been so hot and liquid moments before, went cold and rigid. "Oh no," she whispered.

She shoved the gearshift to Park and grabbed the phone. There were numerous voice messages from her mother and two text messages, both from Raina. One read YUR MOTR IS CRZY TO FND U. CALL ME!!!! The other read 911! I LIED TO HR. Kathleen glanced at the dash clock and saw that it was almost one, well after her curfew. With fingers shaking, she dialed Raina, praying that her friend was still awake and waiting for the emergency call.

Raina answered on the first chirp of her phone. "Where are you? Are you all right?"

"I lost track of time," Kathleen said. "What did you say to Mom?"

"The first time she called, I told her you were here but in the bathroom with cramps. That's when I left the first text message. She called thirty minutes later, and I told her you'd run out for a heating pad because we didn't have one. Oh, yes, and some ice cream too."

Kathleen groaned. "What am I going to tell her? I never lie to her!"

"Sorry . . . I just didn't know what else to say."

"It's not your fault. I'm going home. I'll talk to you tomorrow."

"Wait! Did you have a good time with Carson?"

"Oh, yes." The warmth of Kathleen's earlier feelings washed over her. "Got to go." She ended the call and gunned the engine.

Every light in her home was blazing when Kathleen arrived. She found Mary Ellen sobbing on the sofa, the phone in her lap. "Where have you been? I was getting ready to call the police!" Her mother's eyelid twitched uncontrollably and her speech was slurred, both signs of extreme stress.

Guilt slammed into Kathleen. Her mother looked small and helpless, tangled in an old quilt, a box of tissue on the floor and used tissues heaped on the coffee table. Her right hand lay curled tightly against her side. She couldn't have made it to her wheelchair by herself in the state she was in. What if she'd tried and fallen?

"I'm sorry. I—I just lost track of time." Kathleen sat on the edge of the table and tried to take hold of her mother's good hand, but Mary Ellen pulled away.

"I called Raina and she said you'd gone to the store. Didn't she tell you I called? What's the matter with you? Don't you know how worried

I've been? And you out driving! I thought you'd had a wreck. Like your dad and me. Why couldn't Raina have driven her own car to the store? Why didn't you call me?"

The questions came so fast and furious that Kathleen couldn't begin to answer any. She tried to soothe Mary Ellen, but she was distraught, unconsolable. Kathleen eventually went to the medicine cabinet and found her mother's bottle of tranquilizers. "Take this and we'll talk tomorrow," she said. "I'm sorry, Mom. Really, really sorry."

It was two-thirty before Kathleen crawled into her bed, her mother finally calmed enough to fall asleep. Kathleen lay trembling in the dark, hot tears brimming in her eyes. She'd acted selfishly tonight and had allowed Carson's kisses to lull her into thinking she had a chance at a normal life. It was a mistake. Mary Ellen needed her, depended on her. She was her mother's keeper and sole caregiver. She couldn't ever, *ever* forget that!

Kathleen squeezed her eyes shut, trying to keep tears from leaking out, but she failed. And so she wept alone in her childhood bed. She missed her father horribly. How she longed to crawl into his lap and have him hold her like he used to. She wanted him to tell her everything was going to be okay because Daddy was here to take care of his wife. And his little girl.

thirteen

KATHLEEN AWOKE EARLY the next morning but
stayed in her room as long as possible. She
dreaded facing her mother. It might have been
easier to undo the harm if only Raina hadn't lied
to her! Now she was going to have to deal with
two problems—the failure to communicate her
whereabouts well past her curfew, and the well-
intentioned fib of her friend.

Yet in spite of the mess she was facing, the
thoughts occupied Kathleen's mind most that
morning were of Carson's kisses the night before.
Just the memory made her feel hot all over. Only
yesterday she had been a kissing amateur; today
she felt like a bona fide expert in the art of the
kiss. Practice did make perfect, after all.

She basked in the glow of the memory until
she heard the unmistakable sounds of her mother
banging around in the kitchen. With a sigh,
Kathleen tossed off her covers, slipped on cutoffs
and a tee, and padded into the kitchen. She
watched her mother from the doorway attempt-

ing to make coffee and finally said, "Good morning, Mom. Can I help?"

Mary Ellen flashed her a cold look. "I can do it."

Although the kitchen was wheelchair adapted, Mary Ellen kept bumping into counters. When she spilled coffee filters all over the floor, Kathleen went and picked them up. "Why wreck the place just because you're mad at me?"

"Don't speak to me that way."

Kathleen placed a filter in the coffee machine and scooped coffee into it. "Mom, I don't know what else to say except I'm sorry."

"Why do you even bother to have a phone if you don't keep it with you?"

"I—I don't know. What with the hospital party and all, I just forgot." She guiltily remembered that she'd left it in the car without meaning to.

"And why were you driving Raina's car? Why didn't she go to the store? Especially if you had cramps? And why is it in our driveway this morning?"

Kathleen cringed. She knew she would not be able to continue the lie, yet to confess the truth now seemed even worse. "Listen, I—"

The ringing of the phone saved her. Kathleen grabbed the portable receiver while her mother gave her a disgusted look. It was Raina wanting to know about her car.

"Mom and I are having breakfast, but I'm sure you can stop by in a little bit," Kathleen said pleasantly, hoping Raina picked up on her underlying message. *I can't talk now.*

Raina said, "Can't you drive it over later?"

"I wouldn't count on it."

Raina sighed. "All right. I'll have my mom drop me there. She's not going in till noon today. Will I be allowed in the house?"

"Yes. No one's mad at you." Kathleen told Raina goodbye, then said to her mother, "Raina's coming over later. Can I fix you some breakfast?"

"I'm not hungry."

"Mom . . . you should eat."

When the coffee was ready, her mother poured herself a cup, put it on a tray laid across her lap and rolled toward the doorway. At the door, she tossed over her shoulder, "Maybe I'll just have a bowl of ice cream for breakfast."

"Has she forgiven you yet?" Raina asked. She was sitting on the floor in Kathleen's room while Kathleen sorted through her dresser drawers, tossing out piles of clothing that she'd decided she hated.

"She's still pretty bummed," Kathleen said.

"Does she yell? My mom yells. We have a screaming match, then kiss and make up."

"No. She sulks. And she gets depressed." Kathleen ran out of fevered energy for her project and dropped onto her bed. "I hate upsetting her because I feel guilty about hurting her. She can't take a lot of emotional upheaval, you know. It's difficult for her. Not good for her MS." Kathleen turned toward Raina. "Can I ask you something?"

"Ask away."

"Do you ever miss having a father around?"

The question drew Raina up short because it was so unexpected. Although she and Kathleen were both fatherless, they had rarely talked about it. "Not anymore. It used to bother me. When I was in elementary school and we had parents' night and kids would show up with two parents, that bothered me. By sixth grade, I started to notice that there were other single mothers, so I decided it wasn't so bad. Plus I don't ever remember a dad in the house. I was a baby when mine cut out."

Raina rose, walked to the framed photo of Kathleen's father and picked it up. "But you knew your dad, so I guess it's different for you."

"Very different," Kathleen said, a catch in her voice. "Mom and I both miss him. It's like a dark hole in our lives."

Raina's heart went out to her friend. "I don't even know what my dad looks like. Mom burned their wedding pictures and she told me he hated cameras, so . . ." She shrugged. "And if I sometimes think about him popping back into our lives, I remember Holly and Hunter's dad. I don't think I could stand someone barking orders at me the way he does to them."

Their perception of Holly's father was different. Kathleen didn't see him as dictatorial, but as concerned and caring. "He's not so bad," she said. "You know how Holly exaggerates."

Raina set the photo back on the bedside table. "I used to fantasize about my dad trying to come back into my life. I pictured him coming to the front door and begging Mom and me to take him back and both of us slamming the door in his face."

"I just think about all the things we can't ever do together," Kathleen confessed. "I'll never dance with my father."

Silence settled in the room like a shroud. Kathleen shivered.

Raina stretched her arms above her head. "Well, we've certainly dug ourselves a pity pit, haven't we!"

They looked at one another and laughed self-consciously. "My fault," Kathleen said.

"Then let's talk about something happy. How about your date with Carson? I haven't heard any details yet."

The memory again flooded Kathleen with warmth. "When we got to his house, he took me upstairs to a second-floor balcony overlooking the pool. And we watched the fireworks. They came right up over the trees. It was like our own private show."

Raina looked incredulous. "That's it? You watched fireworks?"

Kathleen sent her a sidelong glance. "Then we made some fireworks of our own."

Raina jumped her friend, put her hands around her throat in mock strangulation and shook her. "You dog! Why didn't you tell me this sooner? Like, you *made out* with him?"

Kathleen laughed and escaped Raina's hold. "For hours," she said. "I thought I was going to sizzle and pop like a firecracker."

"For hours?" Raina looked uneasy.

"Don't panic. He was a good boy . . . kept his hands to himself."

"I'm impressed."

"I wouldn't have let him . . . you know, go any further."

The two girls fell silent. "That's good," Raina finally said. "He should respect you."

Kathleen's face softened. She reached over and laid her hands atop Raina's. "Like Hunter respects *you*," she said. "I won't forget how important it is to be respected."

"Please don't ever forget," Raina whispered.

"So what would you say if I told you I had a boyfriend at the hospital?" Holly posed her question at the dinner table one night while her family were passing bowls of vegetables to one another.

Her father stopped in the middle of dropping green beans onto his plate and eyed his daughter. "I'd say thanks for telling us and then no, you can't have a boyfriend. Not at fifteen."

"But Dad—" Holly was careful to insert a whine of exasperation in her voice while flashing Hunter a look that said, *"Play along."*

Hunter looked confused but said nothing.

"No dating," Mike said firmly. "Did you know about this, Evelyn?"

Holly's mother shook her head. "She's never said a word to me."

"Hunter?"

He shrugged. "I've been on a missions trip, remember?"

"Ben's a very nice guy," Holly said. "How can you judge him without meeting him?"

"I'm not judging this Ben," her father said. "I'm telling you that *you* can't date him."

"Well, too late. We've already had a date," Holly huffed.

"When?" her mother asked. "We would never have given you permission."

"I didn't ask. It was a function at the hospital. You know, that July Fourth party. I didn't think I had to ask permission to go downstairs to a party with him."

"I thought you were in the volunteer program to help the hospital, not to meet boys." Her mother's voice held a reprimand.

"Maybe you should meet him before saying no," Hunter suggested. Holly had told him all about Ben while he had unpacked from his trip.

Holly flashed him a pouty look. She wasn't finished having her fun with their parents yet. She said, "Hunter's right. Dad, why don't you meet Ben before you make me give him up?"

"I don't think meeting him is going to change my mind."

"Of course not. You've already *closed* your mind," Holly said. "Why don't you trust me?"

"It's nothing to do with trust," Evelyn started.

"Then why?"

Mike pursed his lips. "Okay, let's stop this argument before it starts. I'll come meet him."

Holly smiled slyly. "Good. How about Thursday? I have a break at three. Ben and I'll meet you in the cafeteria." She had already received permission from the floor nurse to take Ben to the hospital cafeteria for a snack following his afternoon chemo treatment. Because chemotherapy was often so hard on children, the staff went to extra lengths to ease their discomfort and offer them anything they wanted or were able to eat. She already knew how much Ben loved chocolate cake and had promised him a piece.

"Your father's at work," Evelyn began.

"I can leave early." Holly's father was the leading salesman for his company and had flexible hours.

"Then you can meet Ben. You can too, Mom."

Evelyn shook her head. "Your father can handle this one."

"Your loss," Holly said, and returned to her meal.

Holly stayed with Ben during his chemo treatment in the room set aside for the infusion procedure. She talked to him and read to him during the hour-long process, having promised Mrs. Graham and her friends that she'd be by his side through the ordeal since his mother couldn't, even if it meant going in on days she wasn't working as a volunteer. Holly's presence lessened Ben's apprehension, so it was an easy promise to keep.

"He really likes you," Sue, the charge nurse on the pediatric oncology floor, told her. "Thank you for taking the time to work with him."

On Thursday, while Ben was in the infusion chair with the IV line dripping chemo into the shunt implanted in his small chest, she asked, "We still going for chocolate cake?"

He was fiddling with an electronic toy, scoring points in a Spider-Man game. "I guess. If I don't get sick."

"My daddy wants to meet you, so I invited him to have cake with us."

"Me?"

"He heard we went out on a date."

Ben's little forehead furrowed. "He's not mad at me, is he?"

Holly patted his arm. "No way! He just wants to meet this guy Ben I keep talking about."

"You talk about me?" This seemed to please him.

"All the time."

"Okay. I'll try hard not to get sick," Ben said, returning to his game.

Holly smiled to herself, eager to see the expression on her father's face when he met the boy in her life!

fourteen

HOLLY BOUGHT BEN the biggest piece of chocolate cake on the cafeteria line. She placed his wheelchair by a sunny window in a back corner and sat facing the doorway, and while he dove into the cake, she waited for her father. As soon as she saw him, she stood and waved him over. As he came alongside the table, looking at Ben and then looking perplexed, she said, "Dad, this is Ben Keller," with a beaming smile.

Ben looked up and said, "Hi." Chocolate was smeared all over his mouth, and cake crumbs had fallen onto his hospital-issue pj's.

Holly watched comprehension spread across her father's face. He offered Ben a sheepish smile and held out his hand. "Glad to meet you, Ben."

Ben glanced toward Holly, who said, "Go on and shake his hand. He won't bite."

Ben let his fork drop onto the plate and held out his small hand. Holly's father grasped it warmly. "Holly told me the two of you went on a date."

Ben nodded. "We ate ice cream. I like Holly. She's nice to me."

Holly saw Mike's gaze travel to the gap in Ben's pajama top that revealed the tape used to flatten the shunt to his thin chest, then to the hospital ID bracelet that hung loosely on his wrist. "That cake looks good. Maybe Holly will get me a piece while you and I talk." He gave Holly a five-dollar bill. "You want something else?"

Ben shook his head. "No, thank you. I'm getting full."

Holly could see that Ben was starting to look pale. "Dad, let me take Ben back to his room. I think he needs to lie down," she said quickly.

"I'll wait for you," her father said.

"It may take me some time."

"I'll wait."

Holly needed more than forty-five minutes to get Ben upstairs and resting in his bed because he threw up his cake and had to be cleaned and changed. "I'm sorry," he whispered before she left. "I liked the cake a lot, but my tummy didn't."

"I'll buy you more anytime," she told him. "Get some rest and I'll see you tomorrow."

When she finally rejoined her father in the cafeteria, he had hung his suit jacket on the back of his chair and was drinking a cup of coffee. "Ben got sick," she said, pulling out a chair and sitting. "The chemo, you know. Last time he didn't get sick. You can never tell how it's going to go."

Mike Harrison studied her with his piercing dark eyes. "Why do you do that, Holly?"

"Do what? Help Ben?"

"No . . . why do you go out of your way to jerk my chain?"

"I don't know what you mean." She offered an innocent shrug but felt uncomfortable.

"Sure you do. You could have just as easily told me and your mom about Ben at the dinner table. Why did you make it sound like you were involved with some high school boy when you weren't?"

"You just drew the wrong conclusion."

"No . . . you went out of your way to give the wrong impression."

Holly saw that her father wasn't angry, which was a good thing, but he didn't seem to be taking her little joke very well. She folded her hands in her lap. "I didn't do it to be mean. I guess I just want you to see me like the people around this place see me."

"And how's that?"

"Trustworthy."

"Do you really think that your mother and I don't trust you?"

"Sometimes I wonder." Although she had a laundry list of examples, she didn't want to start an argument.

Mike stirred his coffee. "Please don't confuse house rules with lack of trust. We love you, Holly. We want what's best for you. We take the responsibility of being parents very seriously."

"I know that. I never said you and Mom weren't good parents. All I'm asking for is fewer restrictions. When school starts I'll be a junior, and I still can't pick out the clothes I want to wear." A door of opportunity had swung open unexpectedly and Holly didn't want to let it close while she had her father's undivided attention.

"Is that what this is all about? Wearing clothes we don't approve of?"

"Of course not. It's about me having more freedom."

He didn't say anything right away, just continued to study her, his gaze inscrutable. At long last, he spoke. "When you were little, we made you hold our hand crossing streets. You didn't want to do that and kept tugging away. One time, you sat down in the middle of the street, screaming and trying to break free while cars started coming right at us."

She didn't remember the incident but had to believe him. "What's your point? I know how to be careful now."

"Trust is earned. You can't be given it automatically."

She resisted rolling her eyes. Suddenly this was turning into a lecture instead of a discussion.

"So what you're saying is that you and Mom don't trust me to make smart choices."

"It's not black and white, Holly. And we do trust you. Up to a point."

She wanted to explode but remembered where she was. "Fine," she said, swallowing her anger. "Will you please let me know when I pass the magic point and become one hundred percent trustworthy?"

Mike took a deep breath and stood. "For starters, you can begin by not ever pulling a stunt like this one again."

"What stunt?"

"Using a sick child to get your way."

"But I never—"

"That little Ben isn't a chess piece. I'm glad you've taken an interest in helping him, but don't ever use *anybody* like that again. Manipulation isn't attractive." Mike picked up his suit coat from the back of the chair. "Now, I'll see you at home later. But for what it's worth, permission granted—you can continue to 'date' Ben."

Holly watched her father walk away, his admonition stinging like a slap across her face.

Holly cried later that evening when she recounted the story to Hunter in his room. "It isn't fair! I was just trying to make him see me like others do. Why did he accuse me like that? I'd never do anything to hurt Ben. I'm not using him!"

Hunter held out a tissue box and a wastebasket. Holly grabbed several more tissues and tossed her used ones away. Hunter set the wastebasket on the floor. "I can see Dad's side."

"What! How can you take his side!"

"Don't blow up at me. I'm a sympathetic ear, remember? Think about how it looked to Dad. He goes to the hospital thinking he's got to face you and some boy he's never met, prepared to tell him you aren't allowed to date, and instead he's facing a little five-year-old kid with cancer. That was a big shock to his system. I can see where it might have made him think you were playing a pity card to soften him up."

"I didn't ask him to feel sorry for Ben *or* me. I was just trying to show him that important people—hospital staff—trust me and think I can handle important stuff. No other volunteer has even been allowed on the pediatric cancer floor except me. Not even Raina." She added the last part triumphantly, as if Raina were the measuring stick for trustworthiness.

"This isn't about trumping Raina, is it?"

Holly flushed. "Of course not."

"But Kathleen's dating that Carson guy and I'm dating Raina and Holly is feeling left behind. Am I right?"

She wanted to slug him, but truthfully her brother had gone straight to the heart of the matter. It *was* bothering her that her two best friends had boyfriends and freedom and she had neither. "I hate you," she said, without conviction. She slumped.

Hunter laughed, slung his arm around her shoulders and squeezed. "Your real problem, little sister, is that you're smart and skipped a grade and now you're the youngest in your crowd."

"I'm fifteen," she said defensively.

"Think back. I was sixteen and a half before Mom and Dad let me date. It was just a miracle that Raina even gave me the time of day when I asked her out last year. She was the prettiest girl in the school."

"So what? What are you saying?"

"Someone will come along at the right time for you too. Just be patient. And never stop doing good deeds. I respect the way you're helping Ben."

"You do?" Holly wiped her eyes one more time.

"Raina told me lots of kids have dropped out of the program already, but not you three."

"I like it at the hospital. I like helping. And I really do like Ben. I feel sorry for him, you know, all alone for his treatments. They can be pretty brutal."

"Just think about it, sis." Hunter offered a lopsided grin. "There's only ten years' difference between you and Ben Keller. When you're thirty, he'll be twenty and neither of you will need parental permission to date or even to get married."

She shoved him hard. "This is serious!"

"And marrying Ben isn't?"

She pounced on him, and they wrestled and tickled each other until they were both out of breath and his room was a shambles.

Raina lay stretched out on a float, looking up at the star-studded sky. The water lapped lazily against the sides of the pool in her townhome complex, now deserted because of the late hour. Hunter treaded water beside her, holding on gently to the edge of the float. The sounds of his breathing and the soft splashing of water beneath his free hand lulled her into a warm sense of peace. "I feel like we're the only two people in the world," she said softly.

The pool area was set back from the houses, with high shrubs on one side and the deserted clubhouse on the other. "What would you do if we were?" Hunter asked.

"I'd swim naked in the moonlight," she said.

"And if you did that, we wouldn't be the only two people in the world for long," he joked.

She flicked water on him playfully and turned to face him. "Did Holly get over her bad mood?"

"We had a talk about it. I don't think she figured that Dad would react to her little boyfriend prank the way he did."

"She was steaming when she got into the car the other day, after it happened. Nothing Kathleen or I could say calmed her down."

"She came crying to me too. I got her laughing again, though."

"She's lucky she has a big brother to come to." While they talked, Hunter toyed with Raina's hair, trailing in the water above the top of the float in long, silky tendrils. "Are you sure you have to run off to that camp next month?" she asked. "I'm hardly over missing you from your last trip." The summer was passing quickly and she was dreading his leaving again. Because of their different schedules, she didn't see him nearly enough.

"Yes, I have to go."

She was so close to him that she saw water droplets on his eyelashes. "Will you miss me?" she asked, touching his cheek. Moonbeams fractured the water's surface around them and sparks flared off her heart for love of him.

"I always miss you." He could touch bottom now, so he stopped treading water and stood up.

She slipped from the float and pushed it away, circled her arms around his neck, her legs around his body, wishing she could soak into his very skin. "Do you love me, Hunter?"

"I love you," he whispered.

Raina's insides felt white-hot and she half expected the water around them to boil. They kissed until she felt dizzy. It was Hunter who untangled her legs from his waist and pushed away. "A few more minutes like that and I won't be able to stop myself." His voice was husky and he shook his head, slinging water from his hair. The drops plopped around them like soft rain.

She took deep breaths to slow the pounding of her pulse. "Sometimes I don't want to stop," she confessed, watching him move backward toward the steps.

"Me either. But I want it to be right for us. I want our first time to be right. We'll be each other's firsts," he said, grabbing her hands and pulling her toward the steps with him. "That's worth waiting for, don't you think?"

She stiffened slightly, but he didn't notice. "Yes," she said, feeling hollow inside. "It'll be worth it."

fifteen

KATHLEEN WALKED ON eggshells around her mother for a week, doing penance for her July Fourth escapade. Her mother made no other comments about it, which Kathleen found frustrating. She had fallen out of favor with her mother and she couldn't gauge when she would be forgiven. She felt that they were off balance, out of sync. Perhaps Raina's way was better—yell at each other and get it over with once and for all. Dragging out punishment didn't do her or her mother any good.

To her surprise, Carson called her every night. She longed to be with him. He said he understood when she told him she needed to hang around her house a little while longer. Nor did he act impatient because she wouldn't break her self-imposed exile. Yet when a week had passed, he showed up on her doorstep holding a pizza box and a carton of sodas. "How about me treating you and your mother to dinner tonight?" he said when Kathleen opened the front door.

"Who's here, Kathleen?" Mary Ellen rolled into the foyer. "Oh," she said, seeing Carson. "Hello there."

"Carson Kiefer," he said, introducing himself and offering one of his heart-stopping smiles. "I'm one of Kathleen's friends from the hospital. I brought dinner. And a bag of movies from the video store. Interested?"

Mary Ellen glanced from Kathleen to Carson. "You two can eat without me."

Carson shook his head. "No way. I brought the super king-size, so there's plenty for the three of us. More than enough."

Mary Ellen hesitated and Kathleen held her breath, waiting for the answer. "Are you sure?" she asked.

"Positive."

"Well . . . all right. I'd like to join you."

Buoyed by her mother's receptiveness, Kathleen sprang into action. "I'll make us a salad to go with it. Come on in."

He stepped into the foyer. "No need. I had the pizza place put all that girly stuff on this baby."

"Girly stuff?" Kathleen asked.

"You know, green peppers, olives, mushrooms. Us guys like the other food group—sausage, pepperoni, ham—but I thought, 'Hey, why not toss on some veggies for the women?'"

Mary Ellen laughed. "Go make a salad, Kathleen. I'll set the table. The pizza smells delicious."

In the kitchen, Kathleen grabbed salad fixings from the refrigerator and a large wooden bowl and began tearing up lettuce leaves. Her mother drifted to the table and set out placemats and plates. To Kathleen's surprise, Carson set to work chopping celery and carrots. "I'll do that," she said.

"What—you think I've never made a salad before? Why, I'm known as the Salad King at my house."

"But you're a guest."

"I don't want to be a guest," he said. "I want to be one of the help."

In no time, the bowl was heaped with greens and diced vegetables, the pizza was sitting on the table and cola had been poured into tall ice-filled glasses. They sat down and helped themselves to the food. Carson kept up a stream of hospital stories that made them laugh, and Kathleen couldn't help noticing that her mother was eating more than she had in days, which thrilled her. Her own appetite had improved too, and she felt grateful for Carson's impromptu visit.

When they were finished with the meal, Kathleen asked, "What movies did you bring?"

"A bunch. There's some mushy girl flicks, some action ones with cool car chases, and some mysteries—but not the kind with blood and stuff," he added quickly. "Wasn't sure what you'd like, so I just checked out ten."

"Ten!" Kathleen gaped at him, and he shrugged.

"Let's try one of the action ones," Mary Ellen said. "I see enough of the mushy girl movies."

"Sounds good to me," he said.

Mary Ellen asked, "Do you like being a Pink Angel, Carson?"

He looked pained. "Wish they'd call us something else. I don't like pink and I'm no angel." He grinned impishly and winked, making Mary Ellen laugh. "The program's okay," he added more seriously. "Got a whole lot better for me once I got together with Kathleen."

Kathleen flushed with pleasure. "In other words, Mom, he was so bored that I started to look good to him."

"Not true," he countered. "She looked good to me from day one, but she avoided me like I had a serious virus."

He couldn't have made Kathleen feel better. For whatever reason, Carson was going public with his affection for her and she loved hearing it.

They went into the living room for the movie. Except for the sofa, there was one wing-back chair that Kathleen thought highly uncomfortable. Mary Ellen's nest in the corner of the sofa looked well worn and momentarily embarrassed Kathleen. Compared to Carson's home, hers had to look shabby to him. "Mom's got the sofa," she whispered to Carson. "I'll get some big pillows and we'll hit the floor."

"Suits me," he told her.

Kathleen went to help her mother from her wheelchair to the sofa and was shocked when she struggled to her feet. "I can do this," she said, and took the few steps to the sofa cushions. Carson had also advanced to help, but Mary Ellen waved him off. "My legs are weak, but I can still use them."

As her mother settled into the pillows and spread the blanket across her lap, it occurred to Kathleen that her mother didn't want to appear helpless to Carson. She couldn't figure why. Mary Ellen certainly allowed Kathleen to help her. In fact, Mary Ellen had days when she seemed virtually helpless and called on Kathleen continually for aid.

They watched the movie, not that Kathleen followed the plot. It was enough to be sprawled out on the floor next to Carson. When it was over, Mary Ellen climbed back into her chair unaided and said good night.

"Um—do you want me to come to your room with you?" Kathleen asked. She usually helped her mother get into bed.

"I can manage," her mother said cheerfully. "You and Carson watch another movie. Just check on me before you go to bed, all right? Carson, thank you for dinner tonight, and for your company."

"We'll do it again."

Mystified by her mother's rediscovered abilities, Kathleen watched her leave the room, listening to the whir of her electric chair as she headed down the hall. With a confused shake of her head, she asked Carson, "You want popcorn?"

"Sure."

They went to the kitchen and Kathleen shoved a bag into the microwave.

"You went quiet," he said. "Something wrong?"

She quickly smiled. "Nothing. It was just good to see Mom having a good time."

"Watching a movie on the VCR is a good time?" Carson looked baffled. "What does she usually do for fun?"

"Not much."

"Any friends?"

"A few, but she rarely leaves the house anymore."

"And so you stay with her all the time?"

"I'm all she has." Kathleen felt defensive. Her life and her obligations were too complicated to explain to a boy who had almost unlimited freedom as long as he stayed out of trouble.

"What about *your* life?"

Hadn't her mother's doctor asked the same

thing a few weeks ago? "I'm fine with my life. There's no lock on the door, you know. I come and go like you do at your house." Except that they both knew this wasn't entirely true.

"What does she do all day when you're in school or at the hospital?"

"Reads. Watches TV. Oh, and she puts together scrapbooks. She used to work in an office, but not anymore." She used to do a lot of other things, but the MS had slowly robbed her of her motor skills.

"Doesn't seem very time-consuming," he observed.

"It is for someone with MS," she said testily.

The microwave went off and Kathleen jerked out the bag of popcorn, then dropped it as hot steam from one end of the bag burned her. "Ouch!" She put her stinging finger into her mouth.

He stooped and picked up the bag, put it on the counter, then pulled her close and held her. She struggled for a moment but stopped when he stroked her hair and kissed her forehead. "I'm sorry," he said, without clarifying what he was sorry about.

"You're not feeling sorry for me, are you? Because I don't feel sorry for me and neither should you."

He lifted her chin and looked into her eyes. "How can I feel sorry for anyone who defends herself like a cornered cat?"

"So now I'm a hissing cat?"

"I'd better shut up before I dig myself into a deeper hole." He kissed her mouth. "Show me your room," he said in her ear.

"Why?"

"I want to see Kathleen's lair."

Her heart began to hammer. Her room was on the opposite side of the house from her mother's. An intercom connected the two rooms in case Mary Ellen needed her in the night. "It's just a room. And messy too."

"I don't care how messy. I want to see your space so that I can picture you when I close my eyes at night."

She took him into her bedroom. "I'm going to repaint it," she said once he'd closed the door behind them.

"What color?"

"Lime green, I think."

He went to her bed, and she was glad that she'd taken the time to make it that morning. He picked up her pillow and smoothed it with his hand. She experienced a fluttery feeling in her stomach because there was something intimate and sexy about his stroking her pillow. She imagined that he was touching her. "What do you think?" she asked.

He pressed her pillow to his face, inhaling. "About what?"

"The color, lime green. For the walls."

"I think you could choose any color and it would be perfect. You shouldn't be afraid to experiment, you know. It might be fun."

His eyes looked smoky and dark. She'd never had a boy look at her like that before and she found it exciting, a little bit dangerous. She said, "You make it sound frivolous, like it doesn't matter."

"It should always matter."

She wondered if they really were talking about paint colors anymore. "What if . . . I . . . don't like it?"

"Repaint."

"Seems like a lot of extra work. I'd like to get it right the first time." She said it like a confession and felt the familiar color creep across her face. She had told him something very personal about herself, unsure whether he would catch on.

"The first time," he repeated. A flash of understanding crossed his face. "Yes. It should be right the first time."

They stared at each other, only inches apart. She felt vulnerable and exposed, scared too. Without saying the words, he had told her that he wanted to take her to bed. And she had told him she had not had sex before and that she wanted to wait until the time was right.

He placed her pillow back on the bed. "I have an idea. Let's pick out a bunch of colors and paint a swatch of each one on the wall. Then we'll decide which one you like the best. It's the only way to choose, you know. To see all the colors next to each other."

He was telling her he wouldn't push her, that he would wait for her to decide what she wanted to have happen between them. "That will take some patience," she said.

"Patience is a good thing when you want to get it just right," he said.

She nodded and slipped into his arms and they stood that way, locked in an embrace, for a long, long time.

sixteen

KATHLEEN WAITED UNTIL she, Raina and Holly were alone in the elevator moving toward the volunteer assignment room before she casually mentioned that Carson had brought over pizza and movies the night before.

"Is that why that slap-happy look is all over your face?" Raina asked.

"Could be."

"And we rode all the way here talking about my boring life because you didn't see fit to mention this in the car?" Holly asked.

"Well, I didn't want to monopolize the conversation."

Holly looked at Raina, who poked Kathleen in the shoulder forcefully with her forefinger. "Something happened between you two, didn't it?"

Kathleen stepped out of the elevator and into the hallway leading to the volunteer room. "Could be."

The others immediately flanked her. "Spill it," Raina said.

"My mother had dinner with us, but after she went to bed, he asked to see my bedroom. I let him check it out."

"The two of you were alone in your bedroom?" Holly's eyes were saucer-wide. "What happened? Details. I want details."

"We talked," Kathleen said with an innocent smile.

"That's it?" Raina asked.

Holly hissed in exasperation. "Don't you know I live through you vicariously? I look to your life to be exciting, because mine sure isn't." She threw Raina a glance. "And who wants to hear about her escapades with my *brother*—ugh!"

"We just talked," Kathleen said. They had entered the volunteer room and she picked up a pencil and scribbled her name on the sign-up sheet. "Back down to Administration," she said, reading her day's assignment.

"What did you talk about?" Impatience brimmed in Raina's voice. "Do we have to pry every word out of you?"

Kathleen backed out of the doorway. "Paint chips." She grinned, then turned and jogged quickly toward the elevator.

"Paint chips?" Raina and Holly said in unison, looking at each other.

"What's that mean?" Holly asked.

"I think she's been *sniffing* paint," Raina said crossly while scribbling her name on the sign-up sheet. "She's doing this deliberately, you know. Keeping us in suspense all day long."

"Oh, let her keep her little secret another few hours. She'll come clean when she's ready," Holly said. "I'm on Pediatrics today. How about you?"

"They've put me in the medical library." Raina sighed. "Bor-r-r-ring."

Holly offered a sympathetic expression and hurried off to the pediatric floor. She would get the whole story out of Kathleen on the ride home today if she had to sit on her. She arrived in Pediatrics in time for the morning art program, but before she could get started helping to take children into the playroom, Mrs. Graham signaled her into her office. "Yes, ma'am?" Holly said once she'd stepped through the doorway.

The director went behind her desk and began shuffling papers. "Connie wants you over in the cancer wing. It's about Ben."

Holly's heart skipped a beat. Ben wasn't scheduled for a treatment that day. "What's wrong?"

Mrs. Graham looked startled. "Oh, gracious, I didn't mean to scare you. Ben's just fine. But his mother is visiting. And she very much wants to meet you."

* * *

Beth-Ann Keller was small, and though obviously pregnant, thin with light brown hair pulled into a long ponytail and eyes the same pretty blue as Ben's. She wore a skirt and a blouse that looked long out of fashion, and sat in a wheelchair. Holly introduced herself, and Beth-Ann smiled shyly. "I've been wishing to meet you," she said with a Southern accent. "You're all Ben talks about. Says he's your boyfriend."

Holly grinned self-consciously. "Ben's a doll, and I really like him, Mrs. Keller. The boyfriend thing is kind of a joke between us."

"Except for doctors and such, everybody calls me Beth-Ann, so you do too, all right?" She patted her abdomen. "I had to come in for a checkup today and of course to see my little Ben."

"Is everything all right?" Holly realized it was none of her business and that she shouldn't have asked, but Beth-Ann nodded.

"I'm still on bed rest, but the new baby's growing real good. He's just having a little trouble staying put. Wants to come out and get acquainted before it's time to. I wanted to say hi and thank you for taking such good care of Ben. It's real hard leaving him to go through this by himself."

"I'm glad to do it. Like I said, Ben's a sweetie."

"When they told us Ben would have to come back here, I just sat down and cried my heart out.

I knew I couldn't stay with him like the last time . . . what with the new baby and all. It's hard enough for my little Ben to have to go through all that chemo, but to do it alone, without his mama with him . . . well, that was more than his daddy and I could stand."

Watching Beth-Ann's face, feeling her desire to be with her son, Holly felt a lump rise into her throat. "He's been through a lot, but he's very good about it. Hardly ever cries. I go with him for every treatment. I don't want him to be alone either."

"I know. You see, I prayed real hard to the Lord Jesus that he would send my Ben a special angel to watch over him. And he did." Her smile glowed and Holly felt her face redden.

"I'm no angel," she said.

"All angels don't have wings and sit around the throne of heaven," Beth-Ann said with a practical shake of her head. "Some angels walk around right here on earth and help others. So you're an angel to Ben's daddy and me. To my mama too. She came down from Alabama to help out and to take care of me so I can stay in bed mostly. We all think right highly of you."

Beth-Ann's lavish praise was embarrassing Holly. "I do it for Ben."

"He likes the books you read to him, the stories and all. He don't have many books at home. He's a smart little boy. Oh, just so you'll know, I talked with his doctor a while ago and he says that Ben's responding real nicely to the chemo. He's thinking he might be able to send him back home next month."

"Really? That's great news! I'm so glad you told me. I'll have to go back to school at the end of August."

Beth-Ann looked anxious. "You quitting?"

"No way. I'll still be in the volunteer program, I just don't know my new hours yet."

"Then I'm just going to pray to the good Lord that Ben will be well enough to come home before you go back to school. That way, neither one of you will feel like you're letting the other one down."

Holly found Beth-Ann's simple solution heartwarming. Faith like hers put Holly to shame, and she promised herself that she'd pray harder for Ben.

Just then, a heavyset woman came into the waiting room. Beth-Ann called, "Mama, come meet Holly. She's the one Ben keeps talking about."

After another round of introductions, Holly said she had to get back to work. Beth-Ann's mother said that the courtesy van was waiting out front for the two-hour trip back to their home in Crystal River and they should be going. Beth-Ann pushed herself up. "I have to go kiss my boy goodbye." Her eyes filled.

Knowing Ben would be saddened by his mother's leaving, Holly said, "Tell him I'll come by and eat lunch with him. And that I'll bring him a big piece of chocolate cake."

"That boy loves chocolate cake," Beth-Ann's mother said.

"Will you be able to come back soon?" Holly asked.

"My doctor wants to see me in three weeks, but getting a ride is hard. Just happened to hear that the van was coming today, or we'd have had to take a cab."

"That's a costly two-hour ride," Ben's grandmother said.

Holly's heart went out to them.

"Thank you again for watching out for Ben."

"I have to," Holly called as they started out the door. "He's my only boyfriend."

On the ride home, Kathleen told her friends her bedroom story about Carson. Since she didn't think she'd be able to convey the underlying message about sex, she decided to leave it out and only emphasize the part about repainting her walls.

"So now he's your decorator?" Raina asked.

"No, but I thought it was the safest thing to talk about alone with him in my bedroom."

"What did you decide?" Holly asked.

"I'm thinking lime green."

Holly launched into a description of her meeting with Ben's mother, and Kathleen felt relieved. She truly hadn't wanted a grilling about Carson and didn't want input from either Holly or Raina about being cautious before kicking it up to the next level. *If there is a next level,* she reminded herself. With less than a month to go before school started and with the two of them attending different schools, she had no way of knowing whether Carson would remain interested in her. Especially when Stephanie attended Bryce Academy, same as Carson.

Kathleen arrived home to find Mary Ellen feeling depressed and weepy. Remembering how much her mother had enjoyed the meal with Carson, she asked, "Why don't we go out for dinner tonight, Mom? Nothing fancy."

"I'm tired. I don't feel like it."

Kathleen felt the weight of her mother's depression closing in on her, dispelling her happier mood. "You know, Mom, you might feel better if you got out more. Your doctor wants you to check out the MS support group. I'll be glad to take you sometime. You might like it."

"Please don't tell me what I need. I feel lousy and I'm in no mood for a lecture."

Kathleen's feelings were hurt. "I didn't mean to lecture you. It's just that you seemed to have a good time the other night when Carson came over. I just thought—"

"Stop." Mary Ellen looked on the verge of tears. "I—I can't take this right now. I know you mean well, but you have no idea how difficult it is for me to just get up every day."

"I work in a hospital, remember? I see people checking in a whole lot worse off than you are," Kathleen said, feeling her temper rise. "I know you have problems, but sometimes it just doesn't seem like you're interested in helping yourself."

Mary Ellen's face crumpled. "I don't need this, Kathleen. I really don't."

Kathleen watched her mother back up her chair and start toward the living-room door. It infuriated her when her mother wouldn't talk to her. Lately, it seemed that every time she challenged her, Mary Ellen ran away. "Why can't we ever talk? Why can't you try to change things for yourself? Maybe you feel bad all the time because you don't do anything anymore." Kathleen yelled after her but she was talking to empty space now because her mother had fled. Kathleen was furious. How could Mary Ellen have reduced her into a screaming shrew so quickly? That wasn't the way she wanted to be. Not when just minutes before, she'd been so happy. She went to her room, slammed the door and was looking for something to throw when her cell phone rang. She dumped her purse on the bed, found her phone and saw Carson's number.

"Hi," she said, with forced cheerfulness.

"Hi yourself. You sound out of breath."

"Just rushing around my room. What's up?"

"The grand duke and duchess of the Kiefer manor have requested an audience with the two of us."

"Who? What are you talking about?"

He blew out a deep breath. "My parents want you to come to the house for dinner next Saturday night. And they won't take no for an answer."

seventeen

THE DINNER WITH the two Dr. Kiefers and Carson was all Kathleen talked about in the car ride to the hospital the next day with her friends. "This is huge," Kathleen said. "It makes the country club dinner look like a walk in the park."

"I don't see why," Raina said. "You go, you eat—"

"I get grilled."

"Why do you think they're going to grill you? What have you done to get on their radar?"

"Yeah," Holly interjected. "Raina eats at our house all the time and we don't grill her."

Kathleen let out an exasperated snort. "Why would they? The two of you have been friends for years. They already know all there is to know." She was sitting in the backseat and caught Raina's eye in the rearview mirror. "You two are just poking fun at me, aren't you?"

"Serves you right." Raina didn't deny the charge. "After you going all mysterious on us yesterday about you and Carson in your bedroom."

"This is major serious! I need some support!"

Raina glanced over at Holly. "Should we help her?"

"I guess," Holly said with an exaggerated sigh. She looked over her shoulder. "How can we support you, girlfriend?"

"I don't have anything to wear. In fact, what *should* I wear?"

"Carson's seen the sundress, but his parents haven't," Raina said.

Holly made a face. "She can't wear the same dress twice for him. *You* wouldn't. I remember that you'd dated Hunter a month before you ever cycled through in the same outfit."

"Not that he noticed. This calls for serious shopping. Summer clothes are on big discounts, so you should be able to afford something new."

Kathleen knew that Raina was right. She needed to find something eye-popping for herself, and finding it on sale wouldn't break her savings bank. "I'll do it. When?"

"I'm free this afternoon," Raina said.

"Me too," Holly added.

"What if we can't find anything?"

"Then you can go in your birthday suit. That will be a dinner they'll long remember," Raina teased.

"Have no fear," Holly said, crooking her arm to make a muscle. "Mighty Holly is here. We'll get you dressed for the ball, Cinderella."

"Some ball," Kathleen groused. "I'll probably throw up from sheer nerves."

"Which will once again make it a meal no one will forget," Raina said with a wry grin.

As soon as they'd left the hospital that evening, Raina drove Kathleen and Holly to the mall. With Holly leading the charge through several teen-friendly stores, Kathleen was outfitted in no time with a pretty, short flouncy skirt and a mod retro top. Holly also insisted that Kathleen buy sandals with heels—"but not too high," Holly cautioned—and some new jewelry to complement the look. They stopped at a makeup emporium and Raina discovered the perfect shade of lip gloss for Kathleen. A spritzer of a new patchouli-scented perfume completed Kathleen's budget buying spree.

She insisted on treating to milk shakes and fries in the food court. Once they sat down, she said, "Thanks for your help. I don't feel so panicked anymore. I'm still nervous, mind you, but not freaked."

"That's what friends are for," Raina said, dipping a fry into a blob of ketchup.

"All right," Holly said, reaching into the oversized bag that she used as a purse, "now it's time for both of you to do a favor for me." She pulled out a file folder and extracted a few pieces of paper.

"What do you want?" Kathleen asked.

"Your blood," Holly said with a grin.

"Are they having a blood drive at the hospital?" Raina asked. "They do every now and again, you know."

"Not for a blood drive, but a blood sample for registering yourself with the National Bone Marrow Donor Program." Holly leaned forward, her milk shake forgotten. "I talked to Connie and some man with the organ donor program the other day. Do you know how many people are desperate for organs and die waiting for a transplant?"

"Now you want my liver too?" Raina asked.

"This is serious. Lots of patients with blood cancers can be helped with a simple bone marrow transplant. The problem is finding a donor who's compatible. So the bone marrow registry is a way for hospitals all over the country to document potential compatible donors."

"Hold it," Kathleen said, feeling squeamish. "You asked for blood. Marrow comes from inside the bones."

"True. But the marrow makes red blood cells, and that's what a lot of blood cancers attack. So a transplant can fix someone's marrow and get them well again. Think about Ben."

"Would new bone marrow fix him?"

"I don't know," Holly said. "All I know is if I thought I could save him by donating some of my bone marrow, I'd do it in a heartbeat. If you could save someone's life by donating some of your

marrow cells—cells that us healthy people pro-
duce by the zillions—wouldn't you?"

Raina and Kathleen traded glances. "Well,
since you put it that way," Raina said.

Holly beamed at them. "Good. Then here
are some forms. Because we're still minors, we
have to have our parents' permission, which
shouldn't be too hard to get. And because it's
such a good cause, even *my* parents signed the
form!" She feigned shock. "So when you have a
little free time, go down to the lab at the hospital, turn in the form and let the tech draw some
blood. They'll do the appropriate tests and enter
the results into the national registry. That's all
there is to it. Simple, huh?"

"Except for the needle part," Kathleen said.
"I hate needles."

"Don't be a baby. It'll be over in a few sec-
onds," Holly insisted. "I think it would be so cool
to get a call someday telling me I could save
somebody's life."

"What are the odds?"

"Unfortunately, pretty low, according to the
man from donor services," Holly admitted.

"Ben has parents," Raina said. "I'd think
they'd be more compatible than complete
strangers in some registry."

Holly took a long drink of her chocolate
shake. "Actually, if he ever needs a transplant,
his soon-to-be-born sibling probably would be

the best match. Something about DNA from both parents instead of only one. I'm not sure of the genetics, but a donor has to have a specific number of matching factors before a transplant can work."

Kathleen poked Holly's arm. "You could pass a quiz about this BMT business."

"I listened to what the man was saying, that's all." Holly reached over to Raina's bag of fries. "You going to eat those?"

"Help yourself," Raina said. "All this talk about blood is making the ketchup look disgusting."

Kathleen groaned and pushed herself away from the food, but Holly drenched the remaining fries in the red sauce and made a production of eating every last one.

The dining room in Carson's home reminded Kathleen of a great hall in a castle. The walls were hand-painted with murals of Spanish courtyards, mosaic-tiled fountains, and blooming flower beds. The furniture was large, dark and imposing. Silver candelabras and vases of fresh flowers graced the table's wood surface, set with yellow linen placemats and napkins, ivory-colored bone china dishes, sparkling crystal and ornate silverware. "I told Mom we'd rather have pizza in the kitchen," Carson said, sounding apologetic, "but she said no."

Carson's parents had met Kathleen at the front door when he brought her into the foyer. The Drs. Kiefer were an impressive pair, each for different reasons. Christopher Kiefer had a commanding air of self-assurance, salt-and-pepper hair, and electric blue eyes. Kathleen saw instantly where Carson had gotten his good looks. Teresa Kiefer was petite with stylish, short black hair and eyes of deep chocolate brown. She smiled frequently, laughed often and after a few minutes of conversation, Kathleen saw where Carson had gotten his easy charm. They both had the beautiful, well-cared-for hands of surgeons. She thought them a handsome couple.

"I have prepared a traditional Cuban dinner of *frijoles negros, arroz amarillo con pollo,* salad and fresh bread," Teresa explained, passing Kathleen platters heaped with chicken and yellow rice and aromatic black beans.

Kathleen had never tasted such food but spooned everything dutifully onto her plate. "It smells delicious."

"My grandparents came to Miami from Cuba in the sixties fleeing communism," Teresa said. "My parents moved to Tampa when I was a small child, so I have never seen Cuba. But my family has passed down the good food recipes of our homeland."

"Which is one of the reasons I married her," Christopher Kiefer interjected. "My family is from New England, where a boiled potato is considered high cuisine."

The two of them laughed in unison, making Kathleen smile too.

"And I was born in Tampa and I crave pizza," Carson said. "Go figure."

"You do not bring a pretty girl home and feed her pizza," Teresa said, clucking. "It is not civilized."

Kathleen hastily said, "I like the food. I do most of the cooking in my house, so—" She had been about to say, "—*anything's better*," but stopped in midsentence because it didn't exactly sound like a compliment to Teresa's cooking. She cleared her throat. "I like the change," she finished.

"Do you like volunteering at the hospital, Kathleen?" This came from Carson's father.

"Yes. I plan to continue after school starts."

"It's been good for Carson too. He seems more settled since he's been in the program."

"Perhaps it is the company he keeps," Teresa said, with a lift of her brow that made Kathleen blush furiously.

And so the meal went, with Kathleen fielding occasional questions and Carson's parents discussing little details about their profession and their family. She learned that in their practice Christopher concentrated on adult heart patients, while Teresa specialized in pediatric cases. She heard more about Carson's siblings and their successes. To her surprise, Carson didn't say much, and when the meal was over, he asked her to watch a movie with him in the home theater downstairs. Kathleen thanked his mother profusely for dinner.

"It was a pleasure to have you visit us, Kathleen," Teresa said warmly. "Carson does not often bring his friends home for a meal. We hope you will come again."

On the stairway to the home theater and out of his parents' earshot, Kathleen said, "You told me they *demanded* you bring me over for dinner."

"They always want to meet any girl I'm dating. I just speeded up the process and invited you before they asked me to. They like to put their stamp of approval on everything I do." He sounded resentful.

They hadn't come across as controlling to Kathleen, but how could she judge that based on a single dinner? "What if they don't like me?"

"Believe me, you'd know it if they didn't. And if they didn't"—he paused—"then I guess I'd have to sneak around to see you."

"You would do that?"

"Sure I would," he said without hesitation. "I'm not about to give you up. I like you, and I think we could have something special." He took her hands in his, looked her in the eye. "What do you think?"

eighteen

SHE DIDN'T ANSWER. Was he serious? Only teasing? What exactly did he mean by "something special?" "I—I don't know what you want me to say."

He shook his head, looking disappointed. "I keep thinking that someday you'll throw yourself into my arms and tell me you want me too. Maybe I'm asking too much, but I'll probably keep asking because I like a challenge."

She *wanted* to throw herself into his arms but didn't want to act stupid or be unrealistic either. He said clever things, was dripping with charm and charisma, and she'd had very little experience with boys. She didn't doubt that she must be a challenge to him—but what kind of a challenge? And once the challenge was met, then what? "Where's this home theater, anyway?" She withdrew her hands and changed the subject.

Carson started to say something, changed his mind and continued down the stairs.

She followed. Around the corner, she saw

burgundy leather double doors, a reproduction of doors from an old-style movie theater. Above was a marquee, surrounded by a row of lights that read WELCOME TO THE KIEFER THEATER. A movie house popcorn machine stood next to the doors. "Is this for real?"

"Dad's a movie buff." Carson pushed open the doors and lights came up automatically.

Kathleen saw eight custom reclining theater seats facing a red velvet curtain. Carson touched a control panel on a wall and soft music began to play. The curtains parted to reveal a movie screen with a series of titles scrolling slowly down it. "When one grabs you that you want to watch, let me know," he said.

Kathleen was amazed by the room, but knowing that Carson wasn't happy with her at the moment took some of the fun out of the experience. If only she were better equipped to handle her roller-coaster emotions when they were together!

"Look up," Carson said. The domed ceiling was painted midnight blue. He turned a knob and tiny lights winked on, like stars. "Pick a seat. You want popcorn? I'll fire up the machine, if you do."

"I'm still full from dinner."

"This is a good movie." Carson paused on the title of a popular teen flick from a few years past. "Okay with you?"

"Fine." She chose a chair in the center of the back row, not sure if he would even sit next to her.

"Soda? Candy?" He opened a panel along one wall that held a small refrigerator and a wet bar.

"Maybe later."

He extracted a cola and to her relief, settled in beside her. From a handheld electronic device, he lowered the lights and started the DVD player. A full spectrum of sound thundered from every direction out of speakers hidden in the walls. "Don't freak if you feel the seats move," he said above the opening credits. "They're supposed to vibrate with the sound."

All she could think about was how pitiful her little TV and VCR must have seemed to him the night he'd come to her house. Everything about Carson—his home, his family, his experience with girls, his everyday life—screamed to her that she was way out of her league. She scrunched down into the chair and concentrated on the screen.

When the movie ended, Carson raised the lighting level. "Want to see another?"

"Not right now." Kathleen stretched. "So what do you pay the ushers? I may want a job."

"I know the place is over the top, but that's how my dad does things. My friends hang here during football season—there's satellite TV hooked into the mix." He sounded more upbeat now. "Come with me. I'll show you something else." He held out his hand and she took it.

He pushed on a spot on the opposite wall of the theater and a hidden door swung open. Together they stepped into a room that looked lived-in and homey. She saw two desks, each with a computer; an old-fashioned jukebox; a wall unit of electronic equipment; a game table; and a rumpled sofa surrounded by squishy chairs. "This is my room. Through that doorway"—he pointed—"is the bed and bathroom area."

The abundance of his material possessions astounded her. She felt jumpy as she also realized that she'd never been alone with a boy in his bedroom before. She found herself getting sarcastic, as she often did when she was nervous. She said, "Very nice. How do you stay so humble?"

"I date you. It sucks any conceit right out of me," he fired back.

She walked around the room, making a mental inventory. "I guess you're never bored."

"My parents figured that if I had enough stuff, I'd stay out of trouble." He paused and shrugged. "But it didn't work."

Irritated by his ingratitude, she turned on him. "Your parents care for you a lot. I saw that at dinner tonight, and now I see it everywhere I look. Don't tell me you don't believe it."

"I know they care. The trouble is, I don't feel like I fit into this family. I'm not brilliant like my brother and sister. I'm not much interested in a medical career. And believe me, the lives of this whole family revolve around medicine. Strangers with heart trouble get more attention than the rest of us ever did. That's not what I want for myself. So I'm the goof-off, the black sheep."

She had trouble feeling sorry for him. From where she was standing, it seemed that he had everything, not only materially, but in familial support too. Not only were his parents healthy, but he had both of them. An intercom on the wall crackled with his father's voice, startling her. "Son, can you come up for a minute?"

Carson looked annoyed at the interruption. "Sure," he answered into the intercom. Turning to Kathleen, he said, "I'll be right back. Get comfortable."

Alone, Kathleen couldn't resist slipping into his adjoining bedroom. It had an Asian motif and looked serene and expertly decorated in earthy shades of brown, green and black. Bright splashes of red broke up the muted tones. The bed was neatly made and she wondered how many maids it took to keep up the place.

Feeling guilty about snooping, she was about to leave when a group of framed photographs lining a shelf that ran the length of a wall caught her eye. She walked over to examine them. Most of the photos were of his family, and, she assumed, his friends. In some he looked much younger, and she smiled as she saw him morph from riding skateboards to pedaling bikes to driving cars. *Ordinary pictures*, she thought. All except for one. She picked it up. She felt as if her breath were trapped in her lungs as she stared at Stephanie's beautiful, flawless face in a silver frame. Across the bottom Stephanie had written, "I won't forget our special summer. With much love, Steffie."

Kathleen felt a sinking sensation in the pit of her stomach. *Their special summer*. What did that mean? How special was it? Instantly she was swamped by old feelings of insecurity and inferiority. She wasn't pretty or exciting or steeped in sex appeal. She was just plain old Kathleen and she was a stranger here, someone playing make-believe in a world where she didn't belong. Soon school would start and she and Carson would go their separate ways. *Her* special summer with Carson would be over soon enough.

She was sitting on the sofa when he returned. "Mom and Dad got called into the hospital on an emergency. See what I mean about strangers owning their time?" He didn't sound mad, just matter-of-fact. "Anyway, they said to tell you goodbye and asked me to invite you again." He went to the jukebox and punched a few buttons and a contemporary ballad began to play. "So what would you like to do? Watch TV? See another movie? Check out my bedroom?" He smiled at the last suggestion and waggled his eyebrows.

She stood. "I should go home."

His smile faded. "Why? Are you afraid of being alone with me? Afraid I can't keep my hands off?"

"I'm not afraid." But that wasn't entirely true. She *was* afraid . . . afraid of how he made her feel when he held her and kissed her. Of the ending that she knew was waiting for them in the upcoming months. She faked a smile. "Look, I just got back into my mother's good graces. I don't want to spoil it just yet. Help me out, okay?"

He didn't look as if he believed her, but he said, "If that's what you want."

Their eyes met and she felt the ever-familiar sensations of attraction and desire churn inside her. Yet the image of Stephanie and her intimate signature burned her mind like a brand. Her heart hurt. "Yes. It's what I want."

"Hey, Raina—how do you want Dad to cook your burger?" Hunter called from across his family's backyard patio.

"Well done." She was sitting in a lounge chair helping Holly snap green beans. Evelyn was in the kitchen putting the finishing touches on the evening's picnic meal. Mike was flipping burgers on the far side of the deck, wearing an apron that read DANGER: MEN COOKING, while Hunter talked to him.

Raina looked longingly at Hunter. "I can't believe he's leaving tomorrow."

"It's just for a week," Holly said. "Believe me, I won't miss us fighting for the bathroom in the morning." Her bedroom was separated from Hunter's by a shared galley-style bathroom.

"I don't know why he has to go to that dumb camp anyway. Once he gets back, we'll only have two weeks until school starts."

"He's a counselor and he gets to crack the whip over the lowly. He's been looking forward to it since last summer." Holly jiggled the pan of fresh beans. "It'll be fun."

"*You're* not going," Raina said testily.

"It's not my thing. I went once in eighth grade, capsized my canoe and almost drowned. I think they still talk about me because I was such a klutz. Nope, church camp's not for me."

Hunter came over, adding, "She capsized in two feet of water and was never in any danger." He sat next to Raina on the lounger.

"It was scary," Holly said.

"It was embarrassing," Hunter corrected. "There was some guy she was trying to impress."

"Well, he never forgot me, I'll bet."

Hunter said, "Probably not. When she came

up from the water, she had a piece of swamp grass on top of her head and she looked like an escapee from a cartoon." He and Raina laughed together over his description.

Holly picked up the pot of fresh beans. "Yuk it up. I'm out of here," and with feigned indignation, she carried the pot toward the house.

"You're not still miffed about my going off tomorrow, are you?" Hunter asked.

"No, just sad. I'll miss you."

"I'll miss you too." He toyed with her fingers.

"Don't forget. Our Pink Angels banquet is a week from Saturday."

"I won't forget. Holly wouldn't let me. The folks are coming too."

"So's my mom. Even Kathleen's mother is supposed to show."

"How's Kathleen doing with that Carson guy?"

"All right, I guess. She's at his house for dinner tonight. She really doesn't talk about the two of them very much. Holly and I get on her case about it all the time."

"The three of you practically live together. How could you keep any secrets from each other?"

"We don't," Raina said truthfully. "And because we keep each other's secrets, it's what makes us best friends."

He eyed her suspiciously. "You keeping secrets from me?"

"A girl without secrets would be boring."

"So you *are* keeping something from me! I've always thought so." Still, he grinned.

"I'll never tell."

Just then his father yelled, "Burgers are done! Come and get 'em." He carried a platter of hamburgers from the grill to the picnic table.

"Let's eat," Hunter said to Raina. "We'll talk secrets later."

The screen door slammed and Holly and Evelyn emerged carrying platters of corn on the cob, potato salad and freshly steamed green beans. "Let me help," Hunter said, jumping up.

"The pie's on the countertop," Evelyn said.

Hunter headed off to retrieve the dessert.

Within minutes they were seated at the picnic table and had filled their plates. Raina picked up her burger and was just about to take a bite when Mike cleared his throat. "We'll bless the food now."

Embarrassed, she quickly placed the burger back on her plate. "Sorry," she mumbled. She felt Hunter's gaze and regretted forgetting this part of his family's ritual. She bowed her head because it was expected and waited while Mike Harrison thanked God for the food. All the time, she knew that much more than secrets lay between her and Hunter.

* * *

"You're awfully quiet," Carson said to Kathleen. "Didn't you have a good time?"

He was driving her home from the dinner with his parents. "I had a great time. I've just been thinking."

"Uh-oh. When a girl says she's been thinking, it usually means trouble."

She knew she should say something cute but couldn't come up with anything. She couldn't get the thought out of her head that Carson and Stephanie would be able to see each other every day once school started.

He pulled the car into her driveway and turned off the engine. "Tell me," he said. "What are you thinking about?"

"About school starting and getting busy and not having time for each other." She wanted to ask about him and Stephanie but didn't know how.

"That's not going to happen. I promise, you won't disappear from my life."

"Someone else might come along."

"I'll knock his lights out."

The car's interior was dark and the moon had slipped behind a cloud. "Not for *me*. For *you*."

He lifted her chin. "There's no one else I want. How many times do I have to say it?"

She took a deep breath, trying to muster the courage to bring up Stephanie, then noticed something beyond him on her front porch. "That's odd."

"What?"

"The porch light's off. Mom always leaves it on for me."

"Tell me about it. Maybe the bulb's burned out."

"I don't think so." Kathleen got out of the car and went up the walk and onto the porch. The whole house was dark.

By now, Carson was beside her. "Maybe she went to bed early."

"We usually leave some lights on all night in case she needs me," Kathleen explained, fumbling in her purse for her key.

Kathleen unlocked the door and thrust it open. The house was eerily quiet. She quashed the urge to yell for her mother. Carson might be right about her being asleep. She'd been so tired lately, she often went to bed right after supper.

Kathleen hurried toward the kitchen and her mother's room. In the kitchen, only the small light over the stove was shining. It cast long shadows, but in its feeble light, she saw her mother curled up on the floor in a fetal position, her wheelchair tipped against the wall.

Kathleen screamed.

nineteen

CARSON HIT THE light switch, bounded across the kitchen and dropped to his knees beside Mary Ellen. He shouted, "Kathleen, call 911!"

But Kathleen was frozen in place, thrown backward in time to when she was eight. She was standing in this very kitchen, looking up into her daddy's face. She saw his smile, actually felt the pressure of her arms around his neck, the smoothness of his just-shaved cheek against hers, caught the smell of his aftershave, heard her little girl voice say, *"I love you, Daddy. Bring me a present."*

"Of course, princess. You be good for the sitter. Daddy loves you."

"Kathleen! Call 911!" Carson's shout brought her back to the present, but she was paralyzed, unable to make her legs and hands obey his orders. She heard long-ago voices saying, "Your daddy's dead," and heard her mother sobbing in a hospital bed. Yet she also saw Carson bending over her mother's body, feeling for a pulse in her mother's neck.

"No pulse." Carson turned Mary Ellen flat on the floor and began chest compressions.

Kathleen watched, stupefied by fear. The past and the present were like a river flowing through her head and she couldn't move out of the swiftly rising current of dread.

Carson puffed air into Mary Ellen's mouth, pushed on her chest again and felt for a pulse. "I got it!" he yelled. "She's back!"

The words penetrated Kathleen's stupor, galvanizing her into action. She ran to the phone on the wall, punched in 911 and when the operator answered, cried, "My mother's unconscious!" She was able to give her address, all the while watching Carson rub her mother's hands and legs to keep the circulation going. She hung up the phone, dropped to her knees beside her mother's body across from Carson and wrapped her arms around herself.

She felt icy cold, her hands and fingers numb. "Wh-what should I do?" She hardly recognized her own voice.

"Get me a blanket." He kept feeling for her mother's pulse, ready to begin compressions again if necessary.

She hurried to grab a quilt off the sofa and returned. Carson covered Mary Ellen. Her eyes didn't open and she didn't make a sound.

"Don't let her die," Kathleen whimpered.

She heard a racket at the front door and looked up to see three paramedics rush into the kitchen. One said, "I've got it, son." Carson moved back and the man went to work putting a blood pressure cuff on Mary Ellen and breaking open an IV pack. Another man took Kathleen's elbow and gently helped her up. "Stand over here, miss."

Kathleen saw Carson talking to one of the EMTs, telling him how they had discovered Mary Ellen, what he'd done to help her. He moved over to Kathleen, who shivered uncontrollably, and slipped his arms around her.

Kathleen watched the paramedics set up an IV, hook up electrodes to a portable heart monitor and slip an oxygen mask on Mary Ellen's face. They lifted her onto a stretcher. Kathleen's weeks in the volunteer program had made the trappings of medicine look commonplace, and she was oddly comforted by the sight of them because she knew that every piece was intended to save lives. With Carson's arms around her, the cold, hard knot of fear in her stomach began to loosen.

When it was time to leave, she and Carson followed the men and the rolling stretcher out of the house. She was surprised to see her neighbors, dressed in bathrobes and nightclothes, standing on her front lawn, some looking curious, others worried. The whirling red light from the ambulance spread over them, turning their clothes and skin bloodred. She fended off questions and got into Carson's car quickly. He backed out of the driveway, fell in behind the ambulance that held her mother's life, and followed the blaring siren all the way to the hospital.

In the emergency room, Kathleen wasn't allowed into the triage area with her mother. She filled out forms while Carson made calls on his cell phone. When they were both finished, they sat and waited. He asked, "You okay?"

She didn't answer his question but asked, "Did she have a heart attack?"

"Hard to say."

"Do you think she'll be all right?"

"We got her help pretty fast."

How could he know that? How long had her mother been unconscious? How long had she lain helpless on the floor? Had she been in pain? "Why don't they tell me something?"

He took her hand. "Listen, I called my father. He's coming to take a look at her."

"But she has a doctor. The nurse called Dr. Sanders."

"I know, but my dad knows hearts. I thought he should check her out."

She felt overwhelming gratitude. If he hadn't been with her, if he hadn't taken control—she started shaking. "I—I should call someone," she said.

"Who? A relative?"

Dismayed, she realized there was no one to call. Her father's parents lived in California and although they saw Kathleen occasionally, they weren't close to her and Mary Ellen. Her mother's mother, who lived in Indiana, wasn't well and her grandfather had died years before. "I—I don't know," she said, feeling more miserable. "Maybe Raina and Holly." She looked at the clock and saw that it was one-thirty. "I—I guess I should wait." Her voice caught.

"Do you want anything? Cola? Coffee?"

He was trying to distract her. "No. Nothing."

"I'm going to get myself a soda," he said. "I'll be right back."

She nodded numbly.

At two-forty-five, the doors of the triage area swung open and Carson's father walked out. Kathleen and Carson were instantly on their feet. "My mother—"

"She's stable and conscious," Dr. Kiefer said.

Relief made Kathleen's knees go weak. "Can I see her?"

"In a minute. I want to talk to you first." She and Carson followed Dr. Kiefer to a small room with a table and chairs. Without preamble, he said, "I'm admitting her to the heart unit upstairs, to critical care."

"Was it a heart attack?" Kathleen's own heart was hammering so hard that it felt as if it would leap from her chest.

"Not exactly. We've got to run some tests, but I suspect that she's got a faulty valve in her heart."

"The MS?"

"Actually, I believe it's a congenital defect that's just now presenting. Has she been tired lately? Maybe short of breath?"

Kathleen nodded. All this time she'd thought her mother was just using exhaustion as an excuse to not help herself.

"Carson told me that even after he got her heart beating, her lips and nail beds looked blue, which means she wasn't getting enough oxygen in her blood. That's common with this kind of valve problem."

"Can . . . can you fix the valve?" Kathleen's voice trembled.

"We can replace it," Dr. Kiefer said. "It's major open-heart surgery and having MS isn't to her benefit—but," he added when Kathleen's eyes filled with tears, "I believe we can do it."

Tears spilled down Kathleen's cheeks. "Please save my mother, Dr. Kiefer. Please, don't let her die."

He patted her hand and turned to his son. "I'll get Mrs. McKensie settled, then you bring Kathleen up."

Carson nodded.

"The EMT said you performed CPR and got her heart started."

"I did."

"Hopefully she wasn't unconscious for long."

"I don't think she was," Carson said. "She responded pretty quickly."

"Yes, she's responding well." Dr. Kiefer left the room.

"Why is that important?" Kathleen asked.

"Brain damage can occur if someone's too long without a heartbeat. The brain needs oxygen," he told her gently.

A new fear turned Kathleen icy cold.

"But don't think about that," Carson said. "She's alive and that's what matters."

Kathleen shut her eyes, wishing that this terrible night would end.

"I'll stay with you for the rest of the night," Carson said.

She was grateful. More than anything, she didn't want to be alone.

They were standing near the elevator when the automatic doors of the emergency room opened and a group exploded into the waiting area. Kathleen saw Raina and her mother, Vicki, and Holly and Hunter and their parents heading straight for her. She looked up at Carson.

"I called them," he said. "I think you need them."

The group swarmed around her, firing questions. Mike Harrison shushed them all and opened his arms. Tearfully she stepped into the welcoming embrace of a father's arms. The others encircled them like a pride of lions protecting one of its own.

"Mom says you can stay with us until this is over," Holly said.

"My mom told me the same thing," Raina said.

They were sitting with Kathleen in the hospital cafeteria the next morning. Mary Ellen was settled in the heart unit and resting comfortably. Raina and Holly had remained with Kathleen for the rest of the night. Carson had gone home at seven, promising to return after lunchtime. Kathleen felt tired but much less apprehensive. "That's nice of you," she told both her friends. "I don't know what I'm going to do later on, but if I'm not here, then I want to stay at home. Maybe after the surgery . . ." The sentence trailed off as tears welled in her eyes.

"Has it been scheduled?"

"Dr. Kiefer said it might be as early as Wednesday, maybe Thursday. It depends on what the tests show."

Raina said, "Well, according to my mom, he's the best heart surgeon around."

"I know," Kathleen said. "Open-heart surgery is just so scary. What if she's not strong enough?"

"Don't think that way," Raina said.

Kathleen sniffled.

"I have an idea," Holly said. "Why don't I go home with you and stay while you take a nap."

"I don't have a car here."

"I do," Raina said. "Mom and I came in separate cars."

"Can I drive her home?" Holly asked, perking up considerably.

"No way," Raina said. "I'll take Kathleen home and you go explain to Connie why three of her best Pink Angels won't be reporting for duty today."

Kathleen hesitated. "I don't want to leave Mom."

"Come on," Raina said, urging her up. "Go home, take a hot shower, wash your hair, pack a few things and drive the van back here so you'll have wheels when you want them."

Of course, Raina's suggestion made perfect sense. Sometimes it was good having a take-charge kind of friend.

Kathleen's house seemed unbearably sad and lonely. It was all she could do to walk through the place. The sight of her mother's empty wheelchair in the kitchen, of the debris left behind by the paramedics and of the quilt Carson had used to cover her mother made her cry. The memory of Mary Ellen's body on the floor was a wound carved in her mind and heart. Raina said, "Go take your shower. I'll clean up and put things away."

Kathleen did as she was told, but once she was showered and changed she told Raina she could leave, that she was going to take a short nap and then return to the hospital. Raina didn't argue and as soon as she drove off, Kathleen went straight to her mother's room. She hoped being in the room would comfort her, make her feel safe again. But the empty bed, the lingering scent of her mother's perfume, even the slant of sunlight through the drapes left a terrible aching heaviness inside her.

Beside the bed stood a tall stack of books, all with bookmarks, meaning none had been read to the end. On a long table under a window lay Mary Ellen's scrapbook projects, with partly designed pages, colored-paper cutouts, stickers, a stack of photos, various marking pens, rulers and scissors. A row of low-hanging pegs along one wall kept Mary Ellen's nightgown, robe and a few articles of clothing within easy reach of her wheelchair. Directly across from the bed hung a formal portrait of Mary Ellen and Jim McKensie from their wedding day, eighteen years before. How young they looked! How happy.

Kathleen might have fallen apart except that

the front doorbell rang. Thinking it must be an inquisitive neighbor, she ignored it. She wanted to be alone. The persistent ringing didn't stop. Kathleen clamped her hands over her ears. Minutes later, she heard rapping on the kitchen door. Resenting the intrusion but realizing that the person wasn't going away, she went to the back door and saw Carson through the glass panes, looking worried.

She yanked open the door. "Sorry, I didn't know it was you ringing the bell."

"Holly said you'd come home." He stepped inside.

"I'm taking a few of Mom's things to her."

"Let me help."

They returned to the bedroom and Kathleen went about haphazardly gathering items that might bring her mother comfort in the hospital. She began stuffing the items into an old duffel bag. "I know she can't have this stuff now while she's in ICU, but—but . . ." Her voice broke.

Carson was by her side in an instant. "You can take them later." He gently took a framed photo that she was clutching and set it on a dresser. "Your dad?"

Kathleen nodded, tears trickling down her cheeks. "She'll want him with her."

He led her to the bed and eased her onto the coverlet. He propped himself against the headboard and urged her down beside him.

Kathleen didn't resist.

Carson cradled her head against his chest and, smoothing her still-damp, tangled red hair with his fingers, held her against his heart until she cried herself to sleep.

twenty

MARY ELLEN'S SURGERY to replace a faulty valve in her heart was scheduled for early Thursday morning, Dr. Chris Kiefer as chief surgeon and Dr. Teresa Kiefer attending. Kathleen spent the night before in the sleeper chair near her mother's bed, knowing that the OR team would arrive very early to begin prepping Mary Ellen for the hours-long open-heart procedure. Once she went to recovery, she'd remain there until she was stable enough to be returned to ICU, where she'd spend the days it took her to fully recover. *If* she recovered. The surgery took a toll on patients, and Mary Ellen wasn't in the best of health. But Dr. Sanders assured Kathleen that she would be standing by to help manage any complications from the multiple sclerosis. And Dr. Kiefer also said that once the valve was in place and working, Mary Ellen's quality of life would improve greatly.

In the early part of the evening, Carson came by the intensive care unit to wish Mary Ellen well and because she had asked to see him. "I want to thank you for saving my life," she told him. "You knew just what to do." She reached for his hand as she spoke. "I'm very grateful."

"No problem, Mrs. M.," Carson said. "I couldn't have lived all the years I have at my house and not picked up some medical know-how."

"He was wonderful," Kathleen said, standing beside him.

Carson gave a sheepish grin. "The paramedics did most of the work."

"Well, I've been told that your quick actions made the difference," Mary Ellen said. "At the very least, I owe you dinner when this is all over."

"I'll be there." Turning to Kathleen, he said, "And I'll see you tomorrow morning in the surgical waiting room."

"Raina and Holly have already plotted a game plan for the big wait. Their parents are coming too, so we'll have a crowd," Kathleen said.

"Vicki said she'll be in the recovery room personally to supervise my care after the surgery," Mary Ellen said. "I told her she didn't have to do that, but she said she was looking forward to handling a real nursing duty. That's nice of her and I'm grateful."

"Word's gotten around the hospital," Carson said. "You'll have lots of people checking on you."

Mary Ellen looked pleased to know that Kathleen wouldn't be waiting alone. "Holly said that her church is holding a prayer vigil for me. Can you imagine? A group of people I've never met sitting around and praying for me?"

"Whatever helps, we're for it," Kathleen said.

Carson grinned again. "I'd better be going before the nurse throws me out." In the ICU only one person at a time was allowed to visit a patient, but the nurses were bending the rules that night.

"Yes, she'll be in soon to give me my sleepytime pill," Mary Ellen said.

He gave Mary Ellen a thumbs-up signal and, taking Kathleen's hand, stepped out of the glass cubicle with her and into the hall. "You want a sleepytime pill too? I can ask Dad to order one for you."

"No. I just want to be with her. I can sleep after this is all over."

He kissed her forehead. "See you tomorrow. And don't worry. My dad knows what he's doing."

Back in the cubicle, when Kathleen was alone with her mother, Mary Ellen said, "Kathleen, I want to talk to you before that pill arrives."

"I'm listening."

"We need to talk about what might happen if . . . if the surgery isn't successful." Mary Ellen's eyes looked bright with unshed tears.

"Oh, Mom no—"

"Now, I'm not being pessimistic, but it's foolish to not think about the worst-case scenario." Mary Ellen's voice assumed a no-nonsense tone and her expression was one of determination. "First of all, I've already signed a DNR form."

Do not resuscitate. Kathleen was familiar with the form because of her work in the admissions office. It simply meant that the patient didn't want heroic measures to preserve his or her life if there was no reasonable hope of medical recovery. Many people attached the form to their medical records before having surgeries. It was routine. But now the idea left Kathleen feeling weak and sick.

"I don't want to live in a vegetative state," Mary Ellen continued. "I don't want to be any more of a burden on you than I already am."

Kathleen opened her mouth to protest, but her mother wouldn't allow it. "The second thing is that I've given Holly's parents—Mike, actually—temporary power of attorney. My recovery may take months and someone's going to have to pay the bills for us, oversee the house, keep the van running—you know, the day-to-day-living stuff. He volunteered and I know he's the right person for the job."

Kathleen hadn't even considered such details. Her mother had handled these things for years. "All right," she said.

"If I *don't* make it through, I've agreed to let the Harrisons take care of you. You will live with them at least until you're eighteen, so that you can finish high school. Actually, Evelyn suggested this . . . she's a kind, thoughtful woman. Raina's mother volunteered to take you too, but I think the Harrisons are better prepared for such a job. And what with Hunter graduating and leaving for college next year, they'll have space to spare, according to Evelyn."

By now Kathleen's eyes were filling with tears. The deadly seriousness of what she and her mother were facing had slammed into her head-on. If her mother died, she would be an orphan—motherless, fatherless—alone. She was terrified.

"Now, having said all that," Mary Ellen added, taking her daughter's hand, "I want you to know something else. I don't want to die tomorrow. In fact, when I was lying on that kitchen floor, praying for help, before I blacked out, I realized that more than anything in this world, I want to live. I want to see you finish growing up. I want to see your children.

"Maybe I've not often given you the impression that I wanted to go on living, what with the MS and . . . and the loss of your dad." She picked up Jim's photo and pressed it to her breast. "But more than anything, I want to live. And if I do make it, I promise you things will be different for both of us. Dr. Kiefer says I'll feel better. And when I feel better, I'll do more. I promise you that, Kathleen. Because . . . because . . ." Her voice broke. "Because I love you more than anything on this earth."

Kathleen threw herself into her mother's arms and together they wept, but not out of sadness or despair. They wept out of resolve and out of renewed hope, and for the pure joy of their love for each other.

Kathleen remained with her mother as long as she could the next morning, and when the OR transport gurney arrived to take Mary Ellen up for surgery, she reluctantly said, "See you later"—she couldn't bring herself to say the word "goodbye"—and went up to the surgical floor's family waiting room.

Holly and Raina were already there. Wordlessly, they hugged each other. Holly said, "Come see what we've done." She and Raina had shoved a table into a corner along with a couple of chairs and spread out pieces of a jigsaw puzzle. Holly explained, "This baby has three thousand pieces. I bought it just for today. This way, people can take a break from worrying and noodle over the puzzle piece by piece. Believe me, it'll help pass the time."

Raina showed Kathleen a cooler. "And I've squirreled away a stash of sodas and snacks. No need to leave the floor for anything."

"Thank you," Kathleen said, grateful for the two of them. Then they sat down to wait.

The room was rectangular, with clusters of sofas and chairs. A morning news show played on a television set, dog-eared magazines were stacked on tables, and a pot bubbled with brewing coffee. On one table, Kathleen saw a red phone without a dial face or punch pad. This was the phone the OR used to call the waiting room and notify those waiting when a particular surgery was over. Kathleen longed for it to ring for her.

Carson arrived, as did Holly's parents. Vicki came by to tell them when the actual procedure had begun, then left to watch the operation from the observatory. Kathleen sat huddled in a chair, Carson beside her. When he took a bathroom break, Raina said, "I wish Hunter could be here too."

Kathleen remembered he was still at camp. "Does he know?"

Raina nodded. "We talked last night, and I promised to call his cell phone the minute it's over. He said to tell you that all the counselors prayed for her last night and again this morning."

"Holly thinks there's power in prayer," Kathleen said.

"Let's hope she's right," Raina said, looking to see if Holly was anywhere nearby. "I still can't figure out why God lets this stuff happen in the first place. Doesn't seem very godlike to me to let good people go through bad things."

People from the Pink Angels program began to stop by with words of encouragement. Connie and Mike brought in donuts and promised sandwiches at noon. Kathleen's friends and workers from the admissions office also came by. Twice she wandered to the puzzle table, where Holly and her father were hunched over the jigsaw pieces in deep concentration, their fingers touching as they worked together. As she watched them, a lump swelled in her throat. She missed having a father at that moment almost more than anytime before.

Full of nervous energy, she picked up an abandoned newspaper, leafed through the sections and was stopped cold. She was looking at a full-color picture of Stephanie's face from the front page of the Trendsetter back-to-school supplement. Had it only been the month before when she and Raina had stood at the window looking through binoculars at the photo shoot and making wisecracks? High school and wearing the "right" clothes seemed so trivial. Her whole life could change forever by the end of this day.

"What's up?" Carson interrupted her thoughts.

She jumped. "Nothing," she said. "And everything."

He slid the paper from her hands and stared at Stephanie's photo. Kathleen watched him, remembering the framed image of Stephanie in his bedroom. She couldn't read his expression. "Not too shabby for a girl in high school," she said.

His eyes met hers. "Take it from me, there's nothing glamorous about Steffie's life," he said. "Nothing."

Just then, Holly tapped Kathleen on the shoulder. "Sorry to interrupt, girlfriend, but I've got to take off for a while."

"Where?" Kathleen worried that she might have missed something critical while talking to Carson over the newspaper.

Holly's face lit up. "Ben's going home today. I can't let him go without saying goodbye." She looked over her shoulder at her father, then back at Kathleen. "After all, he's the only acceptable boyfriend I've ever known."

twenty-one

HOLLY RAN TO the elevator, punched the Down button repeatedly, gave up and headed to the stairwell. She hit the ground floor and ran down a hallway and through a giant atrium to a second bank of elevators that would take her to the pediatric floor in the next building. She tried the elevators again. "Hurry up," she demanded after hitting the button. She didn't want to miss Ben's leaving.

The afternoon before, he'd talked of how his daddy and mommy were driving over in his daddy's big red truck to take him home. "But Grandma has to stay at my house 'cause there's not enough seats in the truck for all of us. She's making me a cake!"

Holly made it to the pediatric floor and pushed through the double doors of the cancer wing. She saw nurses clustered around Ben, who was sitting in a wheelchair in front of the desk. Holly recognized Ben's mother too. Balloons, looking like a bouquet of lollipops, had been tied to the arm of the wheelchair and danced above the small crowd. When Ben saw Holly rushing toward them, his face lit up. "Holly! You came to see me."

"I wouldn't let my favorite patient go without saying goodbye," she said, bending to give him a hug.

Beth-Ann said, "Charlie, this here's the girl I was telling you about."

Holly said, "Hi" to the big man next to her.

"We're mighty grateful for the way you helped out with Ben," Charlie Keller said.

"He's a wonderful little boy. I loved knowing him," Holly said.

The Pink Angels volunteer assigned to take Ben down to the patient pickup area asked, "You want to take him down, Holly?"

"I sure do. And thanks."

Hospital rules stated that every patient had to be escorted out of the hospital in a wheelchair after checkout. With another round of goodbyes to the nurses on the cancer floor, Holly and Ben's family walked to the elevator, and this time Holly wasn't in a hurry. Beth-Ann and Charlie carried books, toys, flowers and all Ben's hospital gear. Ben was clutching his pirate teddy bear.

"I'm going to miss you," Holly told him. "Who will I eat chocolate cake with?"

"He'll be back for checkups," Beth-Ann said. "We'll look for you when we come."

Except for her swollen abdomen, Ben's

mother looked thin to Holly, and pale. "How are you feeling?"

"Tired, but real happy to have my little boy coming home." She cradled her abdomen. "Only two more months now. Good thing too. I'm worn out just staying in bed all the time."

Holly pushed Ben outside and into the semi-circular driveway designed for patient pickup. Charlie went to get his truck. Beth-Ann also sat in a wheelchair nearby, and Holly crouched in front of the chair so that she could look into Ben's face. "You think of me whenever you read one of those books, okay?"

"I will, Holly." Ben was still bald from chemo and impossibly thin. His big blue eyes tugged at her heart.

"And stay well."

"I *hate* being sick," Ben said emphatically, then added, "Am I still your boyfriend?"

"My one and only."

"Good."

Charlie's red truck pulled up. Ben's stuff had been secured in the open bed, and the radio played a country song. Charlie lifted his son out of the chair and buckled him into the vehicle's backseat. "Nice meeting you," he said to Holly. He and a nurse helped his wife into the truck.

Beth-Ann leaned out the open window and took Holly's hand. "Thank you for all those books you bought Ben. He loves them."

"It was fun hunting for them in the bookstore and figuring out which ones he'd like best," Holly said. She stepped back and, waving, watched the truck drive away. She stood with the empty wheelchair for several minutes, long after the truck had been swallowed up in traffic, the hot afternoon breeze stirring her hair. She felt a peculiar sense of loss and foreboding that sent a shiver through her. *Kathleen's mother!* With a start, Holly remembered what was going on upstairs. She dragged the wheelchair inside the door and ran for the elevators.

At noon, two of the Pink Angels volunteer staff brought sandwiches to Kathleen and her friends. "You should eat something," Holly's mother said kindly, offering Kathleen a sandwich.

"I don't think I can swallow," Kathleen confessed. She looked at the clock for the millionth time. "It's been hours. When do you think it'll be over?"

"Dr. Kiefer said it could take a long time. Don't worry, hon. A lot of people are praying for your mom. I truly believe that's she's going to pull through this."

Kathleen nodded, not trusting her voice, wishing with all her heart that Evelyn's prediction would come true, and quickly.

"When this is over today, please come home with us," Evelyn said. "I'd love to take care of you while your mother recovers. And Holly would be thrilled to have you stay awhile. And we'd love to have you live with us once school starts. Just until your mother comes home."

"That's nice of you."

Carson had walked up, eating a donut. "You can stay at my place. I'll tell my mom, 'She followed me home. Can I keep her?'"

This made Kathleen and Holly's mother smile. Evelyn said, "I'm serious, dear. You're always welcome in the Harrison household."

Holly bounded into the waiting room just as the red phone rang. An elderly man, also awaiting word from one of the operating rooms, answered it. He held the receiver in the air. "Kathleen McKensie?"

Kathleen's mouth went dry. "That's me," she said, taking the receiver and holding it to her ear.

A voice said, "Dr. Kiefer will be there shortly to speak to you. Please go to the room across the hall."

She hung up, her hands shaking. "It's over," she said. "Dr. Kiefer's coming down."

"Do you want us to come with you?" Carson asked.

She nodded and they all went into the smaller room. Moments later, Carson's parents swooped through the doorway. They wore the green surgical garb of the OR and looked imposing, almost godlike. Teresa was holding her surgical mask and Kathleen saw spots of blood on her gown. She offered Kathleen a reassuring smile. "Your mother made it through the surgery just fine. The new valve is in place and your mother's in Recovery."

If Raina and Holly hadn't been holding her hands and Carson hadn't been standing behind her with his hands on her shoulders, Kathleen would have crumpled to the floor. Everyone in the room gave an audible sigh of relief. "Can I see her?" Kathleen asked.

"Not just yet. Someone will let you know when she's been taken up to ICU."

Dr. Chris Kiefer said, "The next forty-eight hours are probably the most critical in heart procedure cases, but I really think she's doing well. And," he added, raising an eyebrow, "I'm impressed that the head of nursing is in Recovery to oversee her care." He looked tired. "We have things we must do now, but I'll be by to talk to you later." He glanced at his son and their gazes held for a long moment.

"Thanks," Carson said softly.

Dr. Kiefer gave a nod and left the room.

Kathleen turned, put her arms around Carson's neck and buried her face in the front of his shirt. She cried, but this time from relief, from pure gratitude that it was over and that her mother was alive.

twenty-two

"I'M SORRY I can't come to your banquet tonight," said Mary Ellen. She was still in ICU with tubes and wires coming out of her body, but the feeding tube had been pulled that morning, so now, although her voice was raspy, she could talk.

"Mom, don't worry, Holly's dad is taping it and you'll get to see the whole thing." Kathleen had come up to visit her mother before the volunteer awards banquet, scheduled to begin soon in one of the hospital's banquet rooms downstairs. "Besides, it could be boring."

"I'd love being bored. I want to go home."

"You will." After her mother was released from the hospital, she would have to go to a rehabilitation facility until she could function on her own. No one could predict how long that would take.

"How are things at the house?"

"Fine. I stop by and check on things every day."

"Do you like staying at Holly's?"

Kathleen thought for a minute. "It's kind of fun being with her family. There's always something going on. TVs blaring, doors slamming, people coming and going. Holly and I are forever fighting Hunter for the bathroom. Yeah. I like it."

"You've never had a normal family life, that's for sure."

"Oh, Mom, what's 'normal' mean, anyway? 'Normal' is whatever we make it."

Mary Ellen grimaced and shifted in the bed. She still had a lot of discomfort. "Are you ready for school?"

Classes began the following Monday. "The school sent my new schedule and I'm making a supply run tomorrow with Holly and Raina."

"How about clothes?"

"I'm all set."

"No . . . take my department store card and buy yourself some new things. You deserve it."

Her mother's offer touched Kathleen. "Well, if that's okay. Holly's a genius with fashion and I know she'll help. I won't spend too much."

"Get what you want. Life's too short to wear ugly clothes."

Kathleen laughed, then caught sight of the time. "I'd better go. I'll come back when the banquet's over. Want me to bring you a piece of cake? Carson's parents donated a huge cake because they're so thrilled that he actually completed the program."

"Just take plenty of pictures," Mary Ellen said. "Go have a good time."

Kathleen saw that her brief visit was taxing her mother's energy. She kissed Mary Ellen's forehead and said goodbye. Out in the hall, she caught the elevator down to the cafeteria and banquet rooms. Carson would be waiting for her, along with her friends and their families. She felt wonderful.

She was halfway across the almost deserted lobby of the cafeteria wing when Stephanie Marlow materialized in front of her. Kathleen stopped short. "You startled me," she said, struggling to regain composure.

Stephanie was dressed to kill in a suede miniskirt and matching thigh-high boots. "I came for the banquet," she said. "From a fashion shoot."

Kathleen felt plain and ordinary in her summer dress.

"Carson invited me," Stephanie said.

The news shocked Kathleen—he'd never said a word to her about it. "Really?"

"Yes, really." Stephanie crossed her arms. "Listen, don't think that just because he's fooled around with you all summer I'm out of the picture. This has happened before, you know. He finds some new little plaything for a few months and keeps himself busy. But he always comes back to me."

The smug, haughty expression on Stephanie's face made Kathleen want to slap her. She thought of all that had happened during the past few weeks, of how her life had been tossed upside down and of how she'd almost lost her mother. And although she had no way of knowing whether she and Carson would last, she couldn't give Stephanie the satisfaction of thinking her hateful little speech had gotten to her. Kathleen glared at the willowy model. "Well, here's a news flash. I'm not Carson's 'plaything' and he's not a boomerang. And if he wants *you*, then he can have you, because you're all flash. I have a party to go to, so please get out of my way."

Stephanie gave her a look of pure venom, but she stepped aside. Kathleen swept past her, heart racing, anger boiling inside her. She paused at the doorway to gather herself before stepping inside the banquet room. People were everywhere—volunteers, their families, staff. She craned her neck, looking for her friends.

Holly and Raina found her. "We're sitting at table five . . ." Raina's voice trailed off. "Whoa. You don't look happy, girlfriend. What's wrong?"

Kathleen quickly told them of her confrontation with Stephanie.

"Why, that b—" Raina stopped herself, remembering where she was.

"It's okay. I'm thinking the same thing," Holly said.

"I can't believe Carson invited her."

Raina made a face. "Why would you believe her? She'd say anything to get back at you."

"I sure don't believe her," Holly said, looking around. "And I don't see her."

Kathleen looked too, and Stephanie was nowhere in sight. Kathleen had no way of knowing whether or not Stephanie had lied, but at least she was gone. "Let's keep this between us," she said. "I want to have a good time, and I don't want to even think about that awful girl."

"What girl?" Raina said, making Kathleen smile.

"Hey, Kathleen, over here!"

She heard Carson call her name. The three girls threaded their way to a long table holding an enormous cake frothy with mounds of pink and white icing and emblazoned with CONGRATULA-TIONS PINK ANGELS! in hot-pink candy letters.

"Think it's big enough?" Hunter asked.

"You're drooling," Raina said.

"I'm hungry," Hunter countered.

"How's your mom?" Vicki leaned around Kathleen's shoulder to speak.

"Wishing she was here."

"Then she must be feeling better," Vicki said with a laugh.

"Come on," Holly said from behind the table. "Dad wants a picture of the three of us with the cake."

"What about me?" Carson asked, mugging.

"He wants an *attractive* picture," Raina said.

Carson grabbed his chest. "*Ow-w.* I've been shot."

"Get used to it," Hunter said, swiping a taste of frosting.

Kathleen went around the table to stand next to Holly. Raina took her place beside Kathleen. They locked arms and posed for Mike Harrison's camera—three smiling Pink Angels, soon to be juniors, best of friends, closer than sisters.

About the Author

Lurlene McDaniel began writing inspirational novels about teenagers facing life-altering situations when her son was diagnosed with juvenile diabetes. "I want kids to know that while people don't get to choose what life gives to them, they do get to choose how they respond."

Her many novels, which have received acclaim from readers, teachers, parents and reviewers, are hard-hitting and realistic but also leave readers with inspiration and hope.

Lurlene McDaniel lives in Chattanooga, Tennessee.

Here's a sneak peek at *Raina's Story*, the second book in the Angels in Pink series.

one

"Is everything all right?" Raina St. James asked as soon as Kathleen McKensie had climbed into the car and shut the door.

"Sure," Kathleen said halfheartedly, turning her head so that Raina couldn't see her eyes filling with moisture. "Everything's fine. It's hard coming here, that's all." She had just toured the inside of her home while her friends waited for her in the car. She'd gone from room to room checking everything out, as she had every day for the past two weeks. Nothing was disturbed. Everything looked orderly and, except for some dust buildup, seemed the same as when she had been living there.

From the backseat, Holly Harrison reached out and patted Kathleen's shoulder. "Your mom won't be in the hospital forever. Didn't you say

Dr. Kiefer was thinking of transferring her to the rehab center this week?"

Kathleen nodded, still gazing longingly out the car window at the front of her home. "It's just that I can't remember one time that my mom wasn't around for a first day of school. Ever since kindergarten."

"Well, we're here for you now, girlfriend," Raina said, backing her car out of the driveway.

"And . . . and I appreciate it," Kathleen said, finding a tissue and dabbing her eyes. She knew that Raina could have gone to school that morning with her boyfriend, Hunter, Holly's brother, but Raina had elected instead to face day one of their junior year with her best friends. Twisting in her seat, Kathleen told Holly, "And I know your mom tried hard to make the day special for us. It was nice of her to make waffles for breakfast because she knows I like them."

For the past several weeks, while her mother recovered from heart surgery, Kathleen had lived with Holly and her family. Because her father had died tragically years before, she and Mary Ellen had only each other. It had been fun being a part of Holly's family, but Kathleen was ready to go home. Only, her mother had weeks of rehabilitation to go through first, and Kathleen had to remain at Holly's.

"Mom lives to force-feed her family," Holly said, bulging her cheeks out in an exaggerated imitation of overeating. "I could have done just fine with cereal. The first day of school always makes me nervous, and when I'm nervous, I get sick to my stomach."

"Not in *my* car," Raina said, glancing in the rearview mirror at Holly. "Day one makes me excited," she added. "According to my schedule sheet, I can meet Hunter between three classes."

"Whoopee," Holly said without enthusiasm. "We get to meet him coming out of the bathroom every morning. Not a pretty sight."

This made Kathleen smile. "It's not that bad, Raina."

"And don't think I'm not jealous about it either." Raina was crazy about Hunter, now a senior at their high school, and she couldn't imagine facing the next year without him when he went off to college. "Speaking of boyfriends, what do you hear from Carson? I guess today's his first day too."

"He called last night," Kathleen said. "To wish me luck." Since Carson Kiefer attended the prestigious Bryce Academy on the other side of Tampa, she didn't expect to see him often. She figured it was only a matter of time before he forgot about her completely. Wasn't that what the nasty-tempered Stephanie Marlow had predicted to Kathleen at the end-of-the-year banquet for the Pink Angels hospital volunteers just a couple of weeks before?

The words buzzed in her memory. *"Don't*

think that just because he's fooled around with you all summer, I'm out of the picture. This has happened before, you know. He finds some new little plaything for a few months and keeps himself busy. But he always comes back to me."

"Why don't you invite him to our first football game next Friday night? You can double with me and Hunter." Raina's voice pulled Kathleen into the present.

"Maybe I will. He told me he likes the two of you."

"Hey!" Holly interjected from the backseat. "What about me? Who will I go to the game with if you all double?"

"Is there anyone you could ask? We could make it a triple date," Raina said.

"As if my father will allow me to date anyone. I'll be an old dried-up prune before Dad ever lets go." Holly rolled her eyes. Mike Harrison was known for his strictness, especially when it came to Holly. Since she was the youngest of her friends and wouldn't be sixteen until mid-May, she knew she was facing another dateless year. "Is it going to be like this all year?" she groused. "You two running off on dates and me sitting home all alone?"

"We still have our volunteer jobs at the hospital," Raina offered. "We'll be together then."

"And don't think I'm not glad about it, but that's only two afternoons a week."

"And on Saturdays, if you want. I know I'm going to volunteer most Saturdays," Raina said. Hunter worked on Saturdays at a fast-food place, so she'd already decided to volunteer at the hospital while he was busy, because it allowed her to miss him less. "What do you say?"

"Count me in," Holly said, still unhappy about her solo status. "Anything's better than hanging around the house being bored and getting into my parents' way."

"I don't think I can commit," Kathleen said. "At least not until Mom's home and I see what her needs are going to be." Even before Carson's father had performed heart surgery on Mary Ellen, Kathleen had hesitated to be away from her mother too long. Because Mary Ellen was a victim of multiple sclerosis and Kathleen was her primary caregiver, much of her mother's care fell on Kathleen's shoulders.

"Well, don't let her tie you down too much," Raina said in a lecturing tone. "You're just now getting a real life."

"Raina . . ." Kathleen's voice held a warning note.

"Just a caution," Raina added quickly. By now they were in front of the high school, and she whipped the car into the student parking lot. "I have to go to the office and get a parking permit for this school year," she announced.

As they walked, Kathleen couldn't help

noticing that Raina waved and nodded to half the population in the halls. She seemed to know everyone. And why not? Raina was pretty and popular. That was the way it had always been. Holly, cute and perky. Kathleen, shy and quiet. How she had ever attracted Carson was still a mystery to her. And even if they didn't last— *please, God, let us last*—she was facing her junior year feeling like a veteran of the dating wars. Through the summer, she'd had a wonderful time with a totally awesome guy, thanks to the hospital volunteer program where she'd first met Carson.

"Here we are," Raina said, looking dismayed at the line snaking from the main office. A second later, she perked up. Along the hallway, a table had been set up, and behind the table sat a teacher. Above him, taped to the wall, was a sign that read PARKING PERMITS. UPPERCLASSMEN ONLY. "Can they possibly be this organized? I'm stunned."

"Go get your permit. I'll wait over here," Kathleen said, stepping out of the stream of foot traffic. She leaned against the wall, wondering how Carson's first day was going. Bryce Academy took Tampa's elite and wealthy, so it probably wasn't as chaotic as Cummings. She longed to hear his voice, see his face. Yet for all his attentions, Kathleen still felt insecure. He could have any girl he wanted. Why had he chosen her? She wasn't beautiful like Stephanie, who also attended Bryce. Stephanie was a model, and her pictures were all over newspapers and magazines. Kathleen caught sight of herself in the plate glass of the case across the hall that housed the school's sports and academic trophies. Her long red hair looked frizzy with the humidity and her shirt was droopy. Maybe it *was* better that Carson went to another school after all and couldn't see her at the moment.

"Got it." Raina waved the permit and decal at Kathleen. "Let's go hook up."

Kathleen fished for her class schedule as they walked. "Umm, it says here that I have geometry first period. How about you?"

"English lit. Lunch at twelve-forty."

"I'll miss you by fifteen minutes."

"Last periods on Tuesdays and Thursdays are our volunteer times. We can meet in the parking lot and all go together. And don't forget—orientation's this Saturday morning. I'll pick you and Holly up. You going to break out of Admissions and record filing?"

"I like it there. No blood." Kathleen wasn't crazy about hospitals, so remaining in the admissions office and working with paper and files seemed logical to her.

"Just remember, we're getting a school credit

this time around, so diversity counts." For Raina, the credit was an unexpected bonus. She'd have worked without it, but the Pink Angels program offered a high school credit if a student volunteered a hundred and forty hours a semester. A volunteer could work more hours if he or she had a parent on staff. Raina's mother, Vicki, was director of nursing, so Raina already knew she'd be at the hospital beyond the requirement for credit.

"The difference between us," Kathleen said, "is that you want a career in medicine, while I just want to graduate from high school and get into a decent college. I volunteer to be with my friends."

Raina sighed. "You're just too honest."

"What's this?" Kathleen asked, seeing Holly barreling toward them, dodging clusters of students along the way. Her face looked pinched and pale, and she was clutching her notebook to her chest with a death grip.

Holly stopped short in front of Raina and grabbed her arm. "Don't go to the atrium."

"Why? What's wrong?"

"You look like you've seen a ghost," Kathleen said.

"Worse than a ghost." Holly's voice trembled. "I've seen the devil himself." She looked Raina in the eye. "I—I'm sorry to have to tell you this, Raina, but Tony Stoddard's back."